AN ARCHANGEL CALLED IVAN

It then suddenly struck Arliva with a feeling of horror that maybe she would never find anyone who would love her for herself.

She wanted the love her father and mother had had for each other which was why he had never married again, although at times he must have been very lonely.

'I just want to be loved for myself,' she thought. 'I don't want anyone who pretends to care for me because they want my money or anything else I possess.'

Yet she could not stop herself worrying that it was something she might never find.

She felt as if her money was encircling her with tight cords that would prevent her from ever knowing the meaning of real love, the love that everyone wanted, the love of a man and a woman simply because he was the other half of herself.

'That is what I want,' Arliva said to herself, 'but because I am so rich it is a gem I will never find. Even if I want to believe a man loves me I will be quite certain that he will be grasping for that great fortune which exists in my name. Oh, please God, what shall I do?'

The prayer came directly from her heart.

THE BARBARA CARTLAND PINK COLLECTION

Titles in this series

AN ARCHANGEL
CALLED IVAN

BARBARA CARTLAND

.com

Barbaracartland.com Ltd

THE BARBARA CARTLAND PINK COLLECTION

Dame Barbara Cartland is still regarded as the most prolific bestselling author in the history of the world.

In her lifetime she was frequently in the Guinness Book of Records for writing more books than any other living author.

Her most amazing literary feat was to double her output from 10 books a year to over 20 books a year when she was 77 to meet the huge demand.

She went on writing continuously at this rate for 20 years and wrote her very last book at the age of 97, thus completing an incredible 400 books between the ages of 77 and 97.

Her publishers finally could not keep up with this phenomenal output, so at her death in 2000 she left behind an amazing 160 unpublished manuscripts, something that no other author has ever achieved.

Barbara's son, Ian McCorquodale, together with his daughter Iona, felt that it was their sacred duty to publish all these titles for Barbara's millions of admirers all over the world who so love her wonderful romances.

So in 2004 they started publishing the 160 brand new Barbara Cartlands as *The Barbara Cartland Pink Collection*, as Barbara's favourite colour was always pink – and yet more pink!

The Barbara Cartland Pink Collection is published monthly exclusively by Barbaracartland.com and the books are numbered in sequence from 1 to 160.

Enjoy receiving a brand new Barbara Cartland book each month by taking out an annual subscription to the Pink Collection, or purchase the books individually.

The Pink Collection is available from the Barbara Cartland website www.barbaracartland.com via mail order and through all good bookshops.

In addition Ian and Iona are proud to announce that The Barbara Cartland Pink Collection is now available in ebook format as from Valentine's Day 2011.

For more information, please contact us at:

Barbaracartland.com Ltd.
Camfield Place
Hatfield
Hertfordshire AL9 6JE
United Kingdom

Telephone: +44 (0)1707 642629
Fax: +44 (0)1707 663041
Email: info@barbaracartland.com

THE LATE DAME BARBARA CARTLAND

Barbara Cartland who sadly died in May 2000 at the age of nearly 99 was the world's most famous romantic novelist who wrote 723 books in her lifetime with worldwide sales of over 1 billion copies and her books were translated into 36 different languages.

As well as romantic novels, she wrote historical biographies, 6 autobiographies, theatrical plays, books of advice on life, love, vitamins and cookery. She also found time to be a political speaker and television and radio personality.

She wrote her first book at the age of 21 and this was called *Jigsaw*. It became an immediate bestseller and sold 100,000 copies in hardback and was translated into 6 different languages. She wrote continuously throughout her life, writing bestsellers for an astonishing 76 years. Her books have always been immensely popular in the United States, where in 1976 her current books were at numbers 1 & 2 in the B. Dalton bestsellers list, a feat never achieved before or since by any author.

Barbara Cartland became a legend in her own lifetime and will be best remembered for her wonderful romantic novels, so loved by her millions of readers throughout the world.

Her books will always be treasured for their moral message, her pure and innocent heroines, her good looking and dashing heroes and above all her belief that the power of love is more important than anything else in everyone's life.

"I have always believed in angels and that a very special Guardian Angel looks after me and guides me all through my life."

Barbara Cartland

CHAPTER ONE
1860

Arliva walked away from the noise and laughter in the ballroom towards her sitting room.

She had just found that she had left her evening bag on the table after dinner and, as she wanted a handkerchief out of it, she must find out where it could be.

She was almost certain that the servants would have taken it into her sitting room and put it on the writing table, as there would be no doubt that it was hers.

It was gold and had been given to her on one of her birthdays by her father.

It had her initials on it in diamonds and contained an attractive powder compact that had been another present, which also had her initials displayed in precious stones.

In point of fact the whole front of the compact was sprinkled with them.

It was just another indication of her wealth.

At her father's large house in Park Lane she was able to hold an evening party at which everyone in the *Beau Monde* was to be present.

Arliva had made a tremendous impact on the Social world from the moment she first appeared in it.

As her father had died when she was just seventeen, she had stayed quietly in the country for a year.

When she appeared this Season, she was nearing nineteen and had completely astounded the Social world.

It was not surprising because she was immensely rich, which, as the Dowagers said to each other was always an 'Open Sesame' to the *Beau Monde.*

She was also extremely beautiful.

It's really most unfair the other *debutantes* muttered amongst themselves that Arliva should have so much to make her the most talked about, the most beautiful and the most successful *debutante* of the Season.

Lord Ashdown, her father, had been a most brilliant diplomat and he had contributed enormously to the huge British Empire presided over by Queen Victoria.

He had been rich and influential before he became a diplomat, but his success then had lain in the fact that his father had been an extremely clever man and he had done a great deal for the countryside he lived in.

When Lord Ashdown had shown, while he was still at Oxford, that he had an exceptional brain and great charm that was the hope and ambition of every budding diplomat his father had wisely insisted that he become proficient in every foreign language.

When he was later offered an apprenticeship to the Secretary of State for Foreign Affairs, the Secretary said,

"He knows more languages than I do and I cannot imagine anyone who would be more useful to us at this or any other moment."

It was then that Lord Ashdown realised that he was in his element.

He travelled from country to country and, because he was handsome and when it suited him flirtatious, a large number of women fell willingly into his arms.

But surprisingly he did not marry.

It was because he enjoyed his life so much as a bachelor he felt he would find himself tied down, however attractive his wife might be, and he would feel confined in a way he was certain he would hate.

He was therefore nearly fifty when he was finally married.

He was extremely happy with his young and very beautiful wife.

Unfortunately and to his and everyone else's great sadness she died during the birth of her first child.

Whilst Arliva was a comfort to her father, he was continually travelling throughout the world and it was not until she was old enough that he took her with him.

The countries they visited and the people they met made a great impression on a girl who was only fourteen years of age.

She learnt to speak almost as many languages as her father and to be friendly with the men and women of every different nation. It was an extraordinary education in a way for an English girl.

But, when her father died, she then realised that her wandering life had come to an end.

She was obliged to settle down in the large country house he owned in Gloucestershire and be given lessons by Governesses, who could teach her very little that she did not know already.

In his years of extensive travelling Lord Ashdown had become even richer than he had been when he had inherited his fortune from his father.

He was interested in so many different things.

The treasures he had brought home from his travels filled the house in the country to the rafters and were an increasing delight to his daughter.

Whenever she saw something for sale which she knew would delight her father, she insisted on buying it, thereby adding to the great collection he had already made.

Arliva was chaperoned after her father's death by his sisters. As he had four of them, they took it in turns to have her either in the house where they lived or to stay at Ashdown Abbey which had been her father's favourite house and which was now hers.

It was not surprising that the stories of the valuable treasures that the house contained and the beauty and worth of its owner reached London long before she set foot in Mayfair.

To claim that she was an overnight sensation at the first ball given for her in London by one of her relatives was to express the situation mildly.

The very fact that she appeared to be so completely unaware of her beauty and her money made her attractive to every man who danced with her.

Naturally it caused her to receive great attention from the Dowagers, who not only wished to marry off their daughters to someone of importance but also to find a rich and charming wife for their sons.

To Arliva it was a new world that she summed up, as she had every other place she had visited, to find out the truth beneath the obvious glitter and the reality behind the diplomatic pretence.

She had learnt so much from her father.

What was most significant was his advice never to frighten people with your knowledge and never to let them feel that you are too clever to enjoy the compliments they undoubtedly will pay you.

Arliva had laughed at the time, but she had noted how astute her father was in dealing with Statesmen from other countries who wanted to obtain something of value from him.

And how he never let them realise that he was well aware what their tricks would be long before they tried to capture him with them.

Arliva therefore acknowledged the varied proposals of marriage that she received demurely and kindly.

At the same time never letting the man who was proposing be aware that she knew what really attracted him was her fortune.

"You are a huge success, dearest," one of her aunts complimented her, "and we are so proud of you. Of course there is no reason at all for you to be in any hurry to marry anyone."

Arliva realised that her aunts had been consulting amongst themselves as to how they could deter fortune-hunters from snatching Arliva away from them.

They need not have worried.

Her father had taught her so much that she knew almost before the man in question asked her to be his wife that he was thinking of piles of gold rather than the light in her eyes.

The one outstanding talent of Lord Ashdown had been the fact that he could sum up the man he was talking to almost immediately he entered the room.

"It's not exactly what he says or what he does," he told his daughter, "it is something that vibrates from him and that is what you have to learn to recognise."

Arliva understood exactly what her father meant.

As she grew older, he had sometimes allowed her be with him when he had a caller that he suspected would sooner or later desire to conduct some vital business with him.

"Now what did you think of that man?" he would ask Arliva when they were alone together.

"I thought that he was very good-looking and well-dressed for the part he wanted to play," she replied.

Her father had smiled.

"Go on," he urged her.

"Then I sensed," she continued, "that behind the complimentary words that he was mouthing to me and the warm welcome he was repeating on behalf of Her Majesty, there was a determination to obtain something from you which he thought you would not immediately be aware of."

"You are quite right," he said, "and you are getting better at it every day. It was something I rather suspected before he came, but which I could see quite clearly once he began to talk on so many different subjects that he thought would blind me to the main reason for his attention."

"At the same time, Papa, we want this country to be our ally and to support Queen Victoria rather than being antagonistic," Arliva pointed out.

"You are quite right," her father agreed. "Equally the danger remains that they wish to extend their borders and they can only do so by invading the countries adjacent to them."

Looking back on that particular day, Arliva learnt what a brilliant diplomat her father was.

How, just as she had used her brain and her instinct when she was dealing with such people, it was something she must do in a small way in the Social world.

She had incredibly already received no less than five proposals of marriage since she had come to London.

Whilst she had been outwardly flattered by their attention, she had known that the men in question did not love her for herself.

'What I really want,' she mused, 'is to be loved for myself and not for all that I possess.'

She had a strong feeling sometimes that her father's enormous fortune was like a high mountain.

It covered her so completely that it was impossible for anyone to see her as herself.

Now, as she opened the door of her sitting room that had once been her father's, she saw that there was only one lamp alight on the writing table.

But glittering beside it was the gold handbag she had left in the dining room.

She walked across the room and picked it up and then she sat down at the table to look in the small mirror of her compact to see if her hair was tidy.

The last dance she had taken part in had been The Lancers and she had been swung around by enthusiastic young men whose undoubted strength had made her limp in their arms.

She was relieved to see that her hair was unruffled and the beautiful pearls round her neck, which had been her mother's, had not moved.

Then, as she placed the compact back in her gold handbag, she heard a voice speak her name.

"So then, do you really mean to propose to Arliva Ashdown?" a woman's voice resonated round the room.

Arliva stiffened.

Then she realised that the voice came through one of the open windows that led onto a terrace overlooking the garden.

She wondered who was speaking.

Then on an impulse, before she heard the answer, she moved a little nearer to the window.

"I *have* to ask her," a man replied.

Then to Arliva's astonishment there was a note of almost desperation in his voice.

"But, my darling one," the woman said, "how can you marry someone else when we are so happy together? I have always believed that God would answer our prayers and somehow you would find enough money to carry on."

"It is hopeless, utterly hopeless," the man sighed. "As you said, we thought things might improve, but the war took too much from the country and too many men. Two of my best farmers have lost everything they owned with the bad spring and it's impossible for me to help them to replace what has gone."

"I realise that," the woman said very softly, "and you have been really wonderful. You have almost starved yourself to help your people."

"But now I cannot pay the pensioners," the man replied, "so they will definitely starve. As you well know yourself, there is no one working on the land and we have hardly a decent horse left to carry us over the estate."

"I know, I know," the woman cried. "But I love you, Charles, and I know that you love me. How can we possibly go on without each other?"

"That is just what I have been asking myself every night," the man called Charles replied. "It will be an agony beyond words, my darling, to leave you, but I have no alternative than to marry Arliva as her aunt wants me to."

It was then that Arliva realised who was speaking.

It was a young man called Charles Walton whose mother had been one of her aunt's bridesmaids and her greatest friend.

She had heard them talk before of the family estate that he had inherited from his father.

It had been doing pretty well until the Crimean War had taken a great number of men who were in the County Yeomanry into the British Army fighting the Russians and indeed the British casualties had been very high.

"I hate wars," Arliva's father had said at the time, "and it has been extremely poor diplomacy on our part for us to become so entangled in this one."

Arliva knew he was right when in the following years the countryside suffered by the loss of the men who had died so bravely in the Crimea.

She knew now that the young man she had been listening to was a near neighbour of hers in the country.

Her father, who had been a friend of his father, had always said that Charles was a very bright young man who would go far if he had the chance.

Now Arliva realised that his only chance had been to try to save his family home and estate.

And, as he had failed, he was to lose the girl he loved as well.

She had a suspicion who she was, but she was not certain.

Then, when a few minutes later he said her name, she recognised her.

"You do have to be brave about all this, Betty, my precious," Charles said. "But I just cannot allow any more deaths in the village. Apart from that, you know as well as I do that the roof is leaking badly and, unless it is repaired, it will undoubtedly collapse and cost a fortune to replace."

There was silence for a moment.

Then Betty asked,

"Is there anything you can sell?"

"Do you imagine," Charles replied, "that I have not walked round the house a thousand times to find something to sell if it is only a piece of china? But the only things left of any value are entailed onto the son I will never be able to afford to have, although I have often dreamt of how wonderful it would be to see him in your arms."

"I have dreamt of that too," Betty said softly, "but I feel that we are giving in too easily."

"I wish I could think the same," Charles went on. "I have thought about selling the pictures even though it's illegal for me to do so."

"If you did, would anyone really be aware of it?" Betty quizzed him.

"They would know immediately. Every month the Trustees make some excuse to visit me. I know it's to see that I have not sold, as they expect me to do, one of the pictures that were the joy and delight of my grandfather or the silver he inherited as a young man and was determined should remain in the family as long as it existed."

Charles spoke with such bitterness that Arliva was not surprised when Betty sighed,

"I am sorry, darling Charles. It's just that I feel like you do that something must be done. But it would be an agony for me to watch you marrying someone else."

"I have to marry Arliva even though she is quite obviously not in love with me and she will appreciate the fact that her father and mine were close to each other. I am quite certain that, if he was alive, Lord Ashdown would have helped Papa when he knew how bad the situation was."

"Could you not just ask Arliva to help you?" Betty enquired.

"You don't suppose her Solicitors and those who control her fortune would encourage her to give it away in large quantities. To get straight, Betty, my dearest one, we need twenty thousand pounds, which is a fortune by any man's calculations."

There was an ominous silence.

Then Betty said in a trembling voice,

"Do you think she will accept you?"

"Because our fathers were so friendly she at least will be more interested in me than in those over-dressed, stuck-up young London bloods, who flutter round her and who she must realise would make, if they married her, very poor husbands."

"And you think you would be a good one?" Betty asked in a voice that Arliva could hardly hear.

"I would behave to her like a gentleman and be a man of my word. At the same time to marry anyone but you, Betty, would be an agony beyond words. It has made me miserable for the past two weeks to even think about it."

"I wondered what was upsetting you. I thought it was just the death of the two old pensioners and the fact that they had died for want of food."

"I know, I know!" Charles exclaimed. "That is exactly what has brought home to me the horror of what is happening on my land and I feel that I am responsible."

"Of course not," Betty said. "How could you help things going so wrong while you were away? I knew how bad it was before you returned, but what on earth was the point of saying so? There was nothing you could do."

"I know," Charles sighed, "and you were wonderful to many of the people especially those who had babies and were not well enough to feed them."

"I would have done much more if I could," Betty murmured, "but, as you know, my Papa is feeling the pinch just like everyone else and we have a struggle to keep our heads above water."

There was a silence and then Betty said,

"I will pray for your happiness and you do know, Charles, that whatever happens, even if we never see each other again, I will never love anyone but you."

"I can say exactly the same," Charles replied in a deep voice. "I love you, Betty, and you belong to me as no one else will ever be able to do. You are part of me, not only my body but my brain, my heart and my soul. They are all yours and no one else could ever take your place."

Again there was silence.

Then Charles said,

"I want to kiss you, darling. I want to kiss you and for a moment at least we can think of each other and no one else. Let's go into the garden so that you can be in my arms and nobody will be able to see us."

He must have risen as he spoke.

Listening, Arliva heard the chairs scrape as they moved away.

As she gave out a deep sigh realising that she had been holding her breath listening to what the two people were saying, Arliva heard a voice outside the door.

However, she did not wish to speak to anyone at the moment.

There were tears in her eyes because what Charles had said had been so moving.

Without really thinking but just because she wanted to be alone for a moment, she slipped down behind the sofa and was sure that if anyone came into the room they would not be able to see her.

It was then she heard a woman's voice say,

"Now this room is empty and I want to speak to you, Simon. There is no point in you not listening to me."

"I think I know what you are going to say," a man's voice replied.

Arliva recognised it as belonging to the young Earl of Sturton.

He had asked her to dance with him several times this evening and she had managed to avoid him.

She had thought him a rather dull young man and had been delighted to find that she was already promised to someone more interesting.

"Shut the door, Simon," his mother, the Countess of Sturton, was saying, "and listen to what I have to say to you."

"I know what you are going to say, Mama," the Earl replied, "and I am quite certain that Miss Ashdown has no wish to marry me."

"Then you have to persuade her to accept you," his mother replied sharply. "I have noticed that you have not danced with her and only asked to do so once or twice."

"She refused me," the Earl said, "just as she would refuse me if I offered her marriage."

"How do you know that?" the Countess asked him. "After all you have an excellent title and I noticed there were not many amongst those men she was dancing with, as you failed to do."

There was silence as if the Earl could not think of anything to say.

"You must realise that we need the money," the Countess continued, "and there is no one else, no one in the whole of London who has more. Wake up, Simon, and be a man for a change!"

The Earl made a sound which was hardly a word but one of disgust.

"You must be aware that we are in debt, you silly boy, and your marriage to that Ashdown girl will solve all our problems. Now you hurry up and propose to her this evening as I have told you to do and for Heaven's sake make your proposal sound attractive."

"It's just a complete waste of time, Mama," Simon persisted sullenly.

"Nonsense! You have a lot to offer with Sturton Castle even though a huge amount of it needs repairing, but then our family goes back for over a thousand years and that is more than most people here tonight can say."

The Countess spoke with a harshness and edge to her voice which seemed to vibrate around the room.

Then Arliva was aware that she had risen from the chair she had been sitting on.

"Now come along, Simon," she urged. "You must insist on Arliva Ashdown dancing with you. Then take her out into the garden and ask her to be your wife. And for goodness sake make her realise how serious this is to you."

Simon could not answer this.

His mother made a sound that Arliva thought was half anger and half frustration.

Then she heard the Countess walk to the door.

"Now do as I have told you!" she repeated sharply.

Her son made no reply, but Arliva heard him close the door.

Then she stood up from behind the sofa feeling that what she had overheard this evening had been in a way degrading and mortifying.

'All they think about is my money,' she reflected. 'It's not a question to them of whether I would be happy or unhappy.'

It was then that it suddenly struck her that it would be her fate – never to find anyone who loved her because she was just herself.

Her father had often told her how he had fallen in love with her mother.

They had become friends from the first moment they had talked together.

"It was when I had left her," he reminisced, "that I knew I had to see her again. There was something about her that made her different from every other woman I had ever met."

He had smiled before he added,

"And I assure you, my darling, I have met a great number in my life."

"I know that, Papa," Arliva had said. "And what did Mama feel about you?"

"She told me afterwards that from the moment she first saw me she thought I was one of the most handsome men that she had ever seen. But she never for a moment dreamt that I would be interested in her because she was so much younger and she dared to say much stupider than the other women surrounding me!"

Arliva laughed.

"I am sure that was not true, Papa."

"No, indeed it was not! Your mother always had something the Scots call 'fey' that tells them instinctively in their hearts what they don't know in their minds."

"What you are really saying," Arliva said, "is that Mama fell in love with you, Papa!"

"So she always told me and I loved her from the first moment I set eyes on her and believed that she was far too young to be interested in an old man like me."

"But she was and you were so very very happy together," Arliva said softly.

"Happier than it is possible to put into words, but we loved each other with our hearts and I have always believed that your mother would have felt exactly the same about me if I had not a penny to my name and just been 'Mr. No One of Nowhere'.'"

"I am sure that's true," Arliva sighed.

She remembered kissing her father and saying,

"That is how I love you, Papa. Just as you are and not because you are rich and successful."

Her father had laughed and put his arms around her.

"That is how I want you to feel," he said. "And one day you must find someone who loves you for yourself and not for anything you possess."

Arliva could almost hear him saying it.

She knew that so far she had not met anyone who had felt like that about her.

She could hardly believe that what she had listened to had not been part of a dream.

Charles wanting to marry her despite the fact that he adored Betty and Simon being ordered by his mother to ask her for her hand in marriage, although she was certain that he did not find her at all lovable.

It then suddenly struck Arliva with a feeling of horror that maybe she would never find anyone who would love her for herself.

She wanted the love her father and mother had had for each other which was why he had never married again, although at times he must have been very lonely.

'I just want to be loved for myself,' she thought. 'I don't want anyone who pretends to care for me because they want my money or anything else I possess.'

Yet she could not stop herself worrying that it was something she might never find.

She could hear the band playing and knew that her guests would be wondering why she was not with them.

Perhaps they would think she was sitting in some secluded corner listening to a man offering her his heart and he was only really giving her his brain which told him that she was very rich.

She felt as if her money was encircling her with tight cords that would prevent her from ever knowing the meaning of real love, the love that everyone wanted, the love of a man and a woman simply because he was the other half of herself.

'That is what I want,' Arliva said to herself, 'but because I am so rich it is a gem I will never find. Even if I want to believe a man loves me I will be quite certain that he will be grasping for that great fortune which exists in my name. Oh, please God, what shall I do?'

The prayer came directly from her heart.

Now that Charles and Betty had gone, she went to the window as if to look up at the sky.

There was a half moon and all the bright stars were twinkling.

"Help me, please help me!" Arliva cried. "I have to find love, but for the moment it's impossible to believe that any man will ever love me for myself."

She was staring at the moon as she spoke.

Then, as the light from it seemed to descend upon the earth beneath, an idea came to her, an idea so strange and so outrageous that she could not believe it possible.

Yet she knew it was what she had asked for in her prayers.

This was the answer.

CHAPTER TWO

Arliva slept well that night despite the fact that she had been very late going to bed.

It had been two o'clock before anyone had thought of leaving what to them was a very good party.

She was glad when at last some of the older guests decided that they were tired and the band played '*God Save the Queen*'as everyone stood to attention.

They all said that it was one of the best parties they had been to in the Season.

Only Arliva knew what trouble she had experienced in keeping away from the Earl, who had been ordered by his mother to propose to her.

He kept turning up every time she was without a partner to ask her to dance and fortunately she was able to stave him off by saying that she had promised someone else.

In fact she managed to avoid dancing with him at all before the party came to an end.

When she climbed into bed, she did not feel sleepy as she had expected.

She lay still thinking of how Charles and Betty had doubtless gone home clinging to each other almost in tears at the thought that they would seldom be able to do this again.

The idea that had come to her when she had left her sitting room was still there at the back of her mind.

But she had to think her present situation over most carefully as her father had taught her to do.

She looked in depth at her problem from what she believed was an impersonal angle.

Finally she fell into a deep sleep.

*

When she awoke, it seemed to her that things were much simpler than they had been the night before.

She dressed and enjoyed a large breakfast.

To the household's surprise she did not want to go riding in Rotten Row. Instead she ordered a carriage as she said that she needed to go shopping.

Her aunt had made it a rule for some time that she would not have her breakfast until ten o'clock. Therefore she had no desire to discuss the engagements of the day until at least an hour later.

As Arliva did not wish to be questioned as to what she was about to do, she ordered a carriage at a quarter-to-ten to go shopping.

"Do you wish that Mrs. Featherstone comes with you, miss?" the butler asked.

She was the housekeeper and Arliva would usually have preferred to take her shopping with her than one of the other maids, who knew nothing about fashion and only stood staring while she purchased something.

"Not this morning," Arliva answered. "I don't have to go far and I know that she is busy clearing up after last night's party."

"A right mess a party always leaves behind," the butler replied, "especially when it's for the young 'uns."

Arliva laughed.

"We will grow old soon enough. You must not stop us being young while we have the opportunity."

The butler smiled.

"It's good for us all to have you here, Miss Arliva," he said. "We gets old and stuck in our ways, as I were sayin' to cook only yesterday. A party, even if it gives us a lot of work makes us feel young again just watchin' you."

"I knew you would understand, Rickards," she said. "At the same time it will take them a while to make the floor as good as it was. I noticed when the guests came in from the garden that some of them brought in sand and even grass on their shoes."

"We'll soon polish it off, miss," Rickards replied confidently.

Arliva laughed again.

She told Rickards, as he saw her into the carriage, to tell the coachman to take her to Bond Street.

When they arrived, she said that she wanted to go first to the bank in Hanover Square.

Coutts Bank, where her father had kept his money, was one of the oldest in London.

When Arliva asked to see the Bank Manager, she was taken immediately to his room.

As she was announced, he then jumped up from his chair and held out his hand.

"This is a great surprise, Miss Ashdown," he said, "and, of course, you are very welcome."

Arliva smiled at him and sat down in the chair in front of his desk.

"I have come to talk to you, Mr. Carter," she said, "about some of the things I require doing immediately and everything I say is naturally confidential."

The Bank Manager nodded his head as if this was too obvious to require a reply.

Arliva went on,

"I want you to write to Mr. Charles Walton and tell him that my father gave you instructions before he died that, if any of his closest friends were in trouble, he would help them out of their difficulties so long as it was not publicised or talked about to anyone else."

The Bank Manager stared at her in surprise, but he did not interrupt.

"I want you to send Mr. Charles Walton the sum of twenty thousand pounds on the condition that he does not convey to anyone who he has received it from."

The Bank Manager gave a gasp.

"*Twenty thousand pounds*, Miss Ashdown! That is a very large sum and, of course, I would have to discuss it with your Trustees."

Arliva held up her hand.

"I told you that this was a private matter between you and me. I have had my father's instructions as to what to do and you must now take mine that it is a matter of complete secrecy and you must make sure that Mr. Walton does not talk about it to anyone else."

"But I don't think," the Bank Manager said, "that this very large sum can be paid without the support and assurance of your Trustees that the sum would be returned within a certain amount of time and naturally I must have their authority to do what you ask."

There was silence for a moment.

Then Arliva said slowly and in a positive way that made every word seem important,

"I don't think, Mr. Carter, that you have read my father's will very carefully. He gave me complete control of my money when I was eighteen, saying that, as I have the brain and intelligence of any man of twenty-one, he

21

intended to grant me exactly the same rights as if I had become of age."

Again there was silence.

Then the Bank Manager said,

"I do remember that, Miss Ashdown, but I do think it is a very large sum which you are giving away without apparently any chance of making it clear that it must be returned."

"What I have obviously not made clear," Arliva insisted, "is that the money is a gift and it comes from my father, who naturally cannot be thanked and I am not to be mentioned in the transaction in any way."

The Bank Manager put his hand up to his head and scratched it.

"I cannot understand why you are doing this," he said at length.

"There is no need for you to understand it," Arliva replied, "you just have to carry out my wishes."

"I must have support," the Bank Manager protested.

"Why?" Arliva questioned. "I have pointed out that the money is mine to do with as I wish. Or rather in this case to do as my father wished."

There was a pause.

As the Bank Manager did not speak, she continued,

"Of course, Mr. Carter, I also have the power, if necessary, to change my bank."

The Bank Manager then drew in his breath and for a brief moment his face seemed to go white.

Then unexpectedly he laughed.

"Forgive me, Miss Ashdown," he said, "but you spoke so like your father at that moment that I almost felt that he was sitting opposite me. Of course I do understand that you are within your rights, but, as you are so young, I feel you don't realise what a large sum of money this is to be disposed of perhaps without thought."

"That is where you are wrong," Arliva asserted. "I have thought this over very carefully. I want to help as I know my father would have done."

There was another silence and then she added,

"Are you ready to do what I ask or must I go elsewhere?"

The Bank Manager laughed again.

"You know quite well that you are bullying me into a submission over which I have no power, as you pointed out, Miss Ashdown, to do anything else but to obey your instructions."

Arliva smiled.

"I thought you would see sense. I will sign the papers, which I am sure you want me to do. I also want one thousand pounds in cash for myself."

"Now that sounds very sensible," he said. "I have read in the newspapers that you are the best dressed and smartest young lady in the whole of London."

"I like to think they are speaking the truth," Arliva smiled. "But now let me have the papers and your word of honour that you will not discuss this with anyone else."

The Bank Manager only seemed to hesitate for a moment before he assured her,

"You now have my word, Miss Ashdown, that the transaction is between you and me. Mr. Charles Walton, who is a very lucky man, will be informed as you have asked me, that the money comes from your father because he and Mr. Walton's father were very good friends."

"That is exactly what I want you to say and no more please," Arliva agreed.

The Bank Manager sent for the papers for her to sign and also for the one thousand pounds she had asked for herself.

When she rose to leave, he said,

"If you will allow me to say, Miss Ashdown, that you are a remarkable young lady. Of course I might have expected your father, who was the most brilliant man I ever met, to have produced you."

"I am sure, like everyone else, you are thinking it's a great pity I was not a boy!" Arliva said.

The Bank Manager laughed as if he could not help it.

"I suppose quite a number of people have thought that when they realised how bright you are," he replied.

"I imagine that they were really thinking it's a great mistake for a woman to have too much responsibility, but so far with your help everything has run smoothly and I am very grateful."

Arliva held out her hand and the Bank Manager took it.

"All I can say, Miss Ashdown, is that your father would be proud of you, especially if he read of the praise and admiration you are receiving in the Social columns of the newspapers."

"I have often wondered if they would say half as much if I was not overshadowed by my father's money and brilliance."

The Bank Manager knew that there was no answer to this and he merely bowed her to the door.

As she was being driven away in the carriage, she thought that Charles and Betty would be hysterical when the money arrived.

They would now be able to marry each other and would never know that it was just by chance she had been in the right place to eavesdrop on their conversation.

She then told the coachman to drive her to a large shop in Oxford Street, where she occasionally bought small items, but not the smart clothes in which she was so much admired as a *debutante*.

He put her down at the front door.

She walked through the shop without stopping and out through the door at the other end of it that led into Cavendish Square.

She walked across the Square to where at the other side there was an Employment Agency for servants.

It was, she knew, where her aunt's housekeeper engaged servants when necessary and the butler had quite recently taken on a new footman from there.

The Agency was on the first floor above a shop that catered for garden implements.

There was no one on the stairs and Arliva stopped to put on a pair of large dark spectacles that she had worn last year in Switzerland, when she had found the blazing sun on the snow almost overpowering.

She took off the pearls she was wearing round her neck that had belonged to her mother and slipped them into her handbag.

She was aware that now she looked very ordinary.

She had in fact chosen, rather to the surprise of her lady's maid, a dark suit which so far she had not worn in the summer.

She had deliberately chosen to wear a very plain hat that was ornamented with two small feathers on one side of it.

She now deftly removed the feathers and put them into her handbag.

She then walked up the stairs.

As it was quite early, there were not many servants waiting to hear of a new job and there were only two boys present, who obviously wanted to be employed in a stable.

She saw at the far end of the room a woman at a very tall desk and walked towards her.

"Good morning, Mrs. Hill," she said. "I have been told by so many people how efficient you are at finding work for those who need it and I am hoping that you will be able to oblige me."

The woman, who was elderly, then adjusted her spectacles and looked at Arliva critically.

"I am always very glad to hear a kind word about myself," she answered. "They always say that they could not manage in Mayfair without me."

"That is exactly what they do say," Arliva replied. "Therefore I am sure that you will be able to find me a place as a Governess."

"Have you had any experience?" Mrs. Hill asked.

"I have, as it happens, travelled over a great deal of the world and I speak five different languages, but I prefer, if possible, to be with young children. I really need a rest from my last situation which was very strenuous."

"I suppose you have references?"

Arliva opened her handbag.

She had actually written them before she went to bed last night knowing that they would be the first thing she would be asked for.

She had been delighted to find that in her father's writing table, which she had looked in before she went up to bed, that there were a number of letters from people of distinction.

It had been quite easy to erase the few words of goodwill and keep the signature on them.

She had three letters with her from titled people and two of them lived in the North of England, who were not likely to come into contact with Mrs. Hill.

Mrs. Hill then read them slowly and was obviously impressed.

"You seem to be very talented," she remarked. "I will be very pleased to find somewhere for you. But first of all you must give me your name."

"My name is Parker," Arliva told her, "and I would like to be accommodated as soon as possible. As I worked very hard in the last place with two girls of seventeen and a boy of twelve, I would like to be with small children for a short time to give myself a rest."

"That should not be too difficult," Mrs. Hill said reassuringly. "Do you mind being in the country?"

"I was just going to say to you that I would want to be in the country and not in a town," Arliva replied. "I find towns very tiring. Also it means that one has little time for riding and enjoying oneself with animals."

"Most young women of your age," Mrs. Hill said, "find the country dull. But I have the very place for you if you don't mind being isolated with children and animals. I understand from the Governesses I have already sent that there is nothing else."

"Where is it?" Arliva enquired.

"It is Lord Wilson's in Huntingdonshire," she said. "He is an old man, but he has his three grandchildren with him. Two years ago their parents were drowned when the ship they were sailing in to America sank in a very rough sea. No one else in the family wanted three children, so his Lordship was obliged to take his grandchildren in and the trouble they've been to him in that the Governesses I've sent to look after them find the place too dull and too isolated."

She gave a little laugh before she added,

"Young women want the excitement of shops even if they can't afford to buy the goods in them. Shops, I do understand, are very rare where Lord Wilson lives."

"Well, I would like to go there," Arliva answered. "I am sure that it will be a rest from the hectic life I have been having recently."

"I only hope you stay a bit longer than the last Governess did," Mrs. Hill said. "She left after only four weeks and that, I can tell you, is a record."

"I promise you I will stay longer than that," Arliva told her. "I would like to go as soon as possible, please."

"Well, here's the address and I'll write at once to his Lordship's secretary who's been bothering me day after day with letters asking me to send them someone. Your wages will be forty pounds a year paid monthly and they'll refund all the expenses you've incurred in travelling there."

"I will definitely go the day after tomorrow," Arliva announced. "I am quite sure, Mrs. Hill, I will be happy with the children. Are they boys or girls?"

"There's a boy of seven, who is his Lordship's heir, and his two sisters who are twins of six years of age."

"I can only say that I am very grateful to you and, of course, I would like my references returned to me when I arrive at Wilson Hall."

"I only hope that you won't be back asking me for another place like all the others I've said goodbye to," Mrs. Hill replied rather harshly.

"I hope not," Arliva said. "I am looking forward to being in the country even if it is rather isolated."

"Well, very good luck to you and I hope you settle down," Mrs. Hill replied. "I don't mind telling you that it's been a real headache finding young women today, who want to be gadding about in a town rather than attending to their pupils."

She spoke sharply and Arliva then appreciated that she must have sent a good number of applicants to this particular place.

At the same time she felt that this position was just what she needed at the moment.

At least no one from the *Beau Monde* would think of looking for her there.

She thanked Mrs. Hill, signed her name on various papers and then went off down the stairs.

She tucked her spectacles away in her handbag and then she hastily put on her earrings and pearl necklace and hurried across the Square.

Her carriage was waiting outside the shop where she had left it and she told the coachman to take her home.

She felt that both the coachman and the footman were surprised that she carried no parcels with her.

But they immediately drove her back to Park Lane, where she found her aunt coming down the staircase very smartly dressed.

"Oh, there you are, Arliva!" she exclaimed. "I was wondering what had happened to you when they told me that you had gone out shopping."

"I went to buy a present for one of the girls whose birthday it is tomorrow," Arliva replied. "But I could not find anything I liked, so I will have to look after luncheon."

"Now, my dear, you must go and change," her aunt suggested. "Surely you must have remembered that we are lunching with Lady Fotheringay today and you look very drab and dowdy in that get-up."

"I dressed in a hurry as I wanted to go shopping," Arliva told her. "I will not keep you long while I change."

"There is no great hurry, dearest, but I want you to look your very best, so do wear that pretty blue dress you wore yesterday. I thought the hat exceedingly becoming."

Arliva smiled at her.

"I promise I will do you credit, Aunt Molly, but I can hardly do more," she replied.

"Of course not," her aunt agreed. "Did you enjoy your party last night?"

"I thought it was one of the best we have given so far – "

They had moved into one of the sitting rooms while they were talking.

Now her aunt glanced at the door before she said,

"The Countess of Sturton talked to me last night. She is very anxious that you should marry her son."

"But I am not at all anxious to marry him," Arliva answered. "He is very dull and whenever I have talked to him I find his conversation, to say the least, is limited."

Her aunt sighed.

"Of course, dearest, he is an Earl and I believe that their castle is very impressive."

"Which is much more than can be said for Simon Sturton," Arliva retorted.

"Well, do be nice to him if he is at the luncheon today," her aunt said. "I can assure you that his mother thinks the world of him."

It was with difficulty that Arliva did not reply that the Countess of Sturton thought the world of money and not particularly of anything else.

"I will go to change," she said. "I am sure you don't want to be late for Lady Fotheringay."

"No, of course not, and do make yourself look very attractive. I cannot think why you ever bought that suit you are wearing, it really has nothing to recommend it and the hat is even duller."

Arliva then remembered that she had not put the little feathers back into the hat, which would make all the difference to it.

But she replaced them when she had taken off the hat and was walking up the stairs, so that the housemaid should not think it strange.

Then she changed into one of her prettiest dresses.

She chose a hat trimmed with pink roses that was as pretty as the sunshine outside in Hyde Park.

When they drove off to the luncheon party, Arliva said,

"It's getting so hot in London, I would really love to be in the country."

"In the middle of the Season!" her aunt exclaimed her voice rising in surprise. "Think how dull it will be. Here you have a party every night and soon it will be time for Ascot. There, I know, you will be the smartest girl of the year."

Arliva wanted to add, 'and the richest', but she bit back the words.

She was not surprised that Lady Fotheringay made a great fuss of her at the luncheon.

A large number of the men paid her compliments and the girls were obviously jealous at the attention she was receiving.

*

'I want to be myself. I want people to like me because I am me,' Arliva mused as they drove back.

Her aunt was babbling on about the party they were going tonight.

Without her saying so, she knew that the Countess of Sturton would be there telling her son once again that he must be charming to her and, of course, propose marriage.

When they reached the house, she said to her aunt,

"I have a headache. I think it's because it is so hot, so I am going up to my room to rest."

"That is a good idea," her aunt replied, "and I am going to rest in mine. Don't forget that you have to look particularly beautiful tonight."

"Why particularly?" Arliva asked.

There was a moment's pause, then her aunt said,

"Because there will be so many people expecting you to shine and I am sure that is what you will do."

Arliva knew that she was still thinking about what the Countess had said to her.

There was no doubt that she had persuaded her aunt that marriage to the Earl would be a course that would really be to her advantage.

'I don't want to marry the Earl. In fact I don't want to marry anyone,' Arliva told herself when she was alone in her room. 'If I do find people who love me for myself, then I will be proud to be their friends, perhaps even to marry a man who is not interested in my money.'

But she knew that as long as she remained the rich daughter of Lord Ashdown, it would be just impossible for anyone not to think of her money rather than herself.

'It's a curse, rather than something creditable,' she said bitterly to herself as she closed her bedroom door.

Then she locked it and began to pack the case she would take with her when she went to Wilson Hall as a Governess.

She packed all the items she wanted which seemed to her more than most Governesses would possess.

Then, locking up the case, she hid it in the dressing room that contained most of her clothes.

She felt that they looked at her almost reproachfully knowing that, although she had bought and paid for them, she would not be wearing them as long as she was so far away from London.

Then she sat down at the writing table in her room.

She wrote a letter to her aunt in which she said that she had been asked away to stay with some of her friends in the country.

She would be away for a week or so, but they were not to worry about her as she felt that she must have a rest from all the exhausting activities of the Season.

It was a very affectionate letter and she thought that because her aunt was not a very bright or clever woman, she would accept the situation as it was and not make a fuss but wait for Arliva to return.

She lay on her bed wondering if she was mad in what she was doing.

Perhaps she should stay and do what everyone else expected of her and that was to enjoy the Season to the full.

Yet her father had followed his instinct in going abroad when people least expected it.

He had visited countries where he was entranced by what he had found, which invariably turned to gold in his hands, although no one had managed to do it before.

She was the same.

She had to seek out challenges for herself.

She had to find an answer to the question that was growing in her mind more and more day by day.

It was not a question of whether anyone liked her for herself or for what she owned.

'I want to be *me*," she reflected. "I want to be a person just like other people who have just enough money to live on, but not enough to throw about or envelop me with a golden halo."

She sat thinking it all over, vividly conscious of her case already packed, until it was time to dress for dinner.

Her lady's maid accompanied by two housemaids brought in her bath and she had it in front of the fireplace, although it was far too hot to need a fire.

Then she put on one of her most spectacular gowns that had come from Paris.

She knew that it would undoubtedly make her the belle of the ball this evening even without her mother's diamond necklace. And there were two diamond stars arranged in her hair.

'As this is my farewell', she thought to herself with a smile, 'I will give them something to talk about.'

As she went down the stairs, she knew that her aunt looked at her appreciatively.

When she arrived at the house where they were to dine, she was not surprised to find that she was sitting next to the heir to his family title who was as yet unmarried.

He was a very charming and intelligent young man called Peregrine.

"I have heard so much about you," Peregrine said as they started dinner, "that I began to wonder if you really existed except in people's minds."

Arliva smiled.

"I know exactly what you have heard about me," she replied, "but I don't want you to repeat it."

"It was very complimentary," he assured her.

"I am sure it was," she said, thinking of her father's money. "It's very kind of people, but strangely enough I have an urge just to be myself without any trappings."

To her surprise Peregrine understood what she was trying to say.

"Forget it," he said. "People are always envious and therefore they talk if you have more of anything than they have. You must not let it spoil you."

"Why should you think it would?" Arliva asked.

"There was just a note in your voice," he replied, "that told me only too clearly that you are tired of being called 'the rich Miss Ashdown'."

Arliva smiled.

"Right at the very first guess. Go to the top of the class!"

"I can quite understand," Peregrine replied, "that you find it a bore when people talk about your possessions. At the same time you know that you would be lost without them."

"Ignored is the right word," Arliva parried.

He chuckled.

"Now you are being too modest, but I understand that the women look at you reproachfully because you have looks, wit, intelligence and, of course, riches."

Arliva laughed at the way he was speaking.

Then she said,

"You must agree it is all too much."

"I would be willing to change places with you," he replied, "if it was possible. Equally don't attach too much attention to what people say or think. Jealousy is a nasty word and people resent someone having too much."

"And that someone is *me!*" Arliva exclaimed.

"Most people would be on their knees thanking God for having it all. Do you really think it's important?

"I can think of many other things that I would much prefer," Arliva replied.

"What are they?" he quizzed.

She shook her head.

"I am still looking for what I want. Just as my father went out to strange places and found things which no one had ever seen before. I think that is what I really want."

"But you are a woman and so it's impossible," he said. "If you take my advice, you will marry some nice fellow who falls madly in love with you, settle down and have a large family and forget that you can pay the bills."

"Unfortunately no one else forgets it," she pointed out, "and that is what I mind."

"I can understand in a way," Peregrine said, "but I assure you that it is far worse when you cannot pay them and very frustrating."

She remembered as he spoke that at one time he had been a penniless young man and he had not been able to go into the Regiment he wanted simply because it was too expensive.

Then his Godfather had left Peregrine a large sum of money because he had no children and so he had known what it was to be poor.

Naturally he was now enjoying being rich.

In a low voice Arliva enquired,

"Are you telling me that the years when you had no money taught you nothing and you merely hated them?"

"I hated not being able to do what I wanted," he answered. "Then when I realised that the gates had opened and everything was possible, I was extremely grateful. In a way the long years of feeling frustrated and neglected were worthwhile as they made me appreciate, as I never would have been able to do, all that I now have."

Arliva smiled.

"That is the right way to look at it, but how do you cope with the people who would have taken no notice of you in the past but now kowtow at your feet?"

"It's not as bad as all that," he replied, "but quite frankly I forget about them. I am just thankful that I can live here at the moment with my parents and enjoy being able to ride beautiful horses that I never believed in my wildest dreams would ever be mine."

Arliva clapped her hands.

"That is the right way to look at it and, of course, the horses are glad to be yours and never stop to count up what you spend on them."

"That is indeed very true," Peregrine laughed, "and in five years' time, when you have had this world at your feet, you will realise that people love you for yourself even though you are suspicious of it. Then you will forget what you are feeling now and just make the best of things as they are. Which I am sure is, in fact, the very best way."

"Of course it is," Arliva agreed. "But I am afraid I want more, much, much more than what you are telling me."

"Come and dance," he said, "and I will continue my lecture."

They then went out of the dining room and into the ballroom where the band was just beginning to play very softly.

They danced round the floor.

Then he said,

"I ought to have attended this ball with my fiancée whom you have not as yet met. We are announcing our engagement next week and I hope that you will be friends with her as I know she will want to be friends with you."

"Why should she want to?" Arliva asked.

"Because she really enjoys meeting people who are different. She has already complained that the people we have had here up to now have been much of a muchness. In fact I have a feeling at the back of my mind that I will find myself sailing for some strange land before we have had time to settle down in our new house."

"She must be charming!" Arliva exclaimed. "Far too many people have no interest outside their own small circle. That, as you know, always ends in boredom."

"It is absurd for you to be talking like this at your age," Peregrine asserted. "I am ten years older than you and I am now going to prophesy that, if you are looking for the stars, you will eventually find them."

He paused for a moment before he added,

"But it is a long haul up into the sky to where they are!"

Arliva laughed, but later when she was going home she remembered what Peregrine had said and thought that perhaps he was right.

Was she completely mad to go off on her own to try to find people who would like her for herself and not for her money?

When she said goodnight, her aunt Molly said,

"You were a great success tonight, dearest. You looked lovely and I was very very proud of you. It's a pity our host is already engaged because he is such a charming young man and I think he would have been a very suitable husband for you."

"Are you really looking for a husband for me?" Arliva asked.

Her aunt smiled.

"How can I help it? Their mothers, their aunts, their cousins all come and tell me that they have exactly the right husband for you and, as soon as you meet him, you will realise it for yourself and fall in love."

"You have not asked yourself if they want to meet me," Arliva countered.

There was a short silence.

And then her aunt replied,

"Of course, my dearest, you are so pretty and so charming that all the men want to meet you."

'Also so rich,' Arliva thought to herself, but did not say it aloud.

Only when she went up to her bedroom and closed the door did she think that whatever her aunt might say and whatever anyone else might say, she was doing the right thing.

She was starting off on a voyage of discovery.

If she failed, she only had to go back and the Social world would be waiting for her with open arms.

'Of course,' she thought, 'I may not find anyone. In which case it will be the same answer, back again to the old routine.'

Yet somehow she knew that she was being guided in the right direction.

Somehow, perhaps by some miracle she would find what she was seeking and could view the world in a very different way from how she was viewing it at the moment.

'Please God help me,' she prayed fervently and felt sure that her prayer would be heard.

CHAPTER THREE

Arliva's alarm that her father had given her a long time ago, which he had bought in France, went off at six o'clock.

She knew that she had plenty of time before she left because she had everything ready last night.

At the same time she took a great deal of trouble in dressing herself in her plainest and most ordinary-looking clothes.

She put on the hat she had worn yesterday from which she had removed the feathers.

Then she gazed at herself in the mirror and felt that her face looked very young.

She carefully drew a line under both her eyes with a pencil and was certain that it made her look at least five years older than she actually was.

She was about to put on her glasses, but thought it might be rather intimidating for the children to see their Governess with huge dark glasses, so she tucked them into her pocket.

She waited until it was nearly seven o'clock when she knew that the whole staff would be having breakfast.

Her aunt, because she was not very strong, did not rise early and she usually rang the bell to be called just before ten o'clock.

So there was no one in the front of the house and when she went to the top of the stairs she saw that the hall was empty.

She found the case she had packed a considerable amount of clothes into was very heavy.

But somehow she managed to get down the stairs, open the front door and walk out as quickly as she could manage it into Park Lane.

She knew there was usually a place where Hackney carriages accumulated and she made her way to it and she was very pleased when she saw ahead that there were quite a number of carriages waiting for passengers.

Arliva's arm was by now aching considerably from the weight of the heavy case.

She stopped at the first one and the driver, who was sitting on the box, turned round to say,

"Can I take you anywhere, miss?"

"I wish to go to King's Cross Station," she replied.

"I'll take you there in a jiffy," he answered cheerily, jumping down from the box and taking hold of the heavy case from her.

He put it behind his seat and then opened the door for her to climb into the carriage.

It smelt rather musty after the very smart carriages her father had always used.

She felt, as she drove away, that she was setting off on a marvellous adventure with golden wings.

'No one will be able to find me for a long time,' she told herself, 'and by then I may well have found all that I am seeking.'

It seemed to her that they reached King's Cross Station in a very short time because she was so deep in her own thoughts.

The driver handed her case down to a porter.

"Where be you goin', miss?" he enquired.

Arliva had the directions that Mrs. Hill had given her and she read them to the porter.

"That 'ere train be in now," he said. "But it won't be leavin' till eight o'clock."

"I am quite prepared to wait," Arliva answered. "So, if you will find me a comfortable carriage, I will be very happy."

The porter laughed.

"It's what all travellers 'opes they'll be and many be disappointed."

She paid the Hackney carriage driver his fare and it included a good tip.

He looked at it in surprise and then said,

"Thank you very much, miss. I 'opes you 'ave a good journey."

"That is what I hope myself," Arliva replied.

She smiled at him before she turned to follow the porter.

He was wheeling her case in his trolley and they walked quite a long way until, in one of the platforms, she saw a small train that was obviously the one travelling to Huntingdonshire.

The porter found her an empty carriage – in fact they were all more or less empty.

He then put her case in the guard's van.

She tipped him and he touched his forelock.

"That be the first I've 'ad today," he said, "and you be a real lady bringin' me luck."

"That is what I am looking for myself," she sighed.

"Then perhaps you'll find it!" the porter exclaimed. "I thinks lookin' as you do you'll win one way or another."

"I can only hope your good wishes will come true," Arliva answered, "and thank you for bringing me here."

She sat down in the carriage and wondered what would happen when the housemaid called her and found her bedroom empty with the letter to Aunt Molly lying on the pillow.

She knew that the older servants would be shocked at the idea of her going out alone so early in the morning as she was always expected to have someone in attendance.

And they would be even more surprised that she had left without travelling in one of the many carriages that belonged to her.

She knew, however, that everything would carry on exactly as it had for the last ten or fifteen years and the same applied to the house in the country.

Her father had chosen very skilful and trustworthy men to be in charge of the house and the estate, just as the older servants, who had been in the house in Park Lane, had been in charge for nearly the same length of time.

'I suppose I am very lucky in having them,' Arliva mused.

At the same time it was yet another of the many attractions that acted as a bait to those men who valued her possessions more than her.

During the next quarter-of-an-hour people began to arrive on the platform and climb into the empty carriages.

Arliva hoped that she would travel alone.

But just before it was time to leave, a young man, who she thought looked as if he was a salesman or perhaps a senior clerk, entered her carriage.

He sat at the other end from where she was sitting and he looked at her once or twice but did not speak.

The train then started to leave with a great deal of puffing and clanking.

They had travelled some way before the young man asked Arliva somewhat tentatively,

"I wonder if you would mind if I smoke. I did not realise when I boarded the train that this one was a non-smoking carriage."

"It will not worry me," Arliva replied.

She thought, as she was speaking, just how many cigars her father had smoked during the day.

She had grown used to the smell of his cigars and he had often said that they helped him to think.

"Not that I would approve of women smoking," he had added quickly. "So I refuse to allow you to even try it."

"I have no wish to do so," Arliva had answered, "but I like the aroma of your cigars."

"I used to buy them when I could afford it," her father replied, "but now I find they help me to think out my plans and I pride myself that, if I have a problem, by the time I have finished my cigar I have solved it!"

"Then, as you have so many problems, Papa, your cigars must always be at hand."

"Absolutely right!" her father had chuckled.

The young man had by now opened his cigarette case and Arliva saw that it was quite an expensive-looking one.

"Can I offer you a cigarette?" he asked.

Arliva shook her head.

"It's very kind of you, but I don't smoke."

"Quite right too," he said. "I don't like women who smoke. They always smell of it and seem to make more mess of smoking than a man does."

Arliva laughed.

"I am sure you are right, but I think that smoking is essentially a man's pleasure and if women smoke there just seems something wrong about it."

She thought as she spoke that some of the Society Dowagers had begun to smoke.

Their contemporaries had been very rude about it, while the younger men had said definitely it spoilt a pretty girl if she smelt of cigarettes and it was not attractive to watch her smoking.

When he had offered her a cigarette, the young man had moved almost opposite her.

Now he asked,

"Where are you going?"

Arliva thought it a mistake to give him her address, so she replied,

"I am getting off at Huntingdon."

"Oh, I know that part of the country," he said. "I think you'll find it very dull."

"I have already been told so," Arliva replied. "But, as I am going to look after children, I should expect that they will keep me busy."

"So you're a Governess!" the man exclaimed.

Arliva nodded.

There was silence for a moment before he said,

"It's only the rich who can afford a Governess for their children. I was sent to school almost as soon as I could toddle and I hated the other children who teased me and knocked me about until I was old enough to hit them back."

"Which I am sure you did very effectively."

She realised that he was nearly six foot tall and had a determined attitude about him and it made her think that he would always get his own way.

"I don't suppose you're interested," he said, "but I've had to fight hard for my place in life and now I've got it I'm really determined not to lose it. That means using my brain twenty-four hours a day."

"What do you do," Arliva asked, "which makes it such hard work?"

"I'm running a business that makes certain products for this country and I am striving in every way possible to encourage a demand for them overseas."

"It sounds exciting!" Arliva exclaimed. "At least you can move about and not stay stuck in one place which might be dull."

"You're quite right," he agreed, "but sometimes I find it very hard when I'm wanted in two or three places at the same time and there's no way of getting there faster than the train will take me."

"Is that what you are doing now?" Arliva asked.

"It is," he affirmed, "so I don't suppose that I'll be seeing you again, which I would like to do."

Arliva looked at him enquiringly.

Then he said,

"You are the prettiest young girl I've seen for a long time and that's a considerable compliment because I see a great many of them one way or another as I travel around."

"Thank you," Arliva answered, "you encourage me to feel that I may be a success in the new job I have just undertaken."

She thought as she spoke how amused her father would be at her doing anything so unnecessary as working for her living.

At the same time she knew it was the first step in her determination to meet people who liked her for herself and not for what she possessed.

Because she thought it a mistake to talk too much about herself, she said,

"Do tell me which countries you are working in at the moment. I have done a little travelling and I always thought that the salesmen in France are more polite and efficient than those in other countries."

He considered what she said before he replied,

"I think you are right. I also find that I get on very well with the Italians, although you have to make sure that they pay up before you deliver the goods."

"That must apply to many countries, but I am sure that you are clever enough to prevent them from tricking you," Arliva commented.

"I try to be," he replied. "But as you doubtless will know the world is full of people who want something for nothing and those who find it more amusing to trick you than to play the game fairly, so to speak."

"I know exactly what you are saying to me," Arliva agreed. "My father thought the same and, when I travelled with him, he always warned me against trusting a foreigner too far and making sure that I received full value for the money I spent."

"Your father was clearly very wise," the man said. "But I think you'll find where you're going the country folk are slow and you'll not find anyone bright enough to trick you even if they wanted to do so!"

"You are very encouraging," Arliva smiled.

The young man was silent for a moment and she sensed that he was considering her in detail as he puffed at his cigarette.

Then he said,

"You are too pretty to be working for your living. Just you watch out for those who'll be after you like a fox after a chicken. Lock your bedroom door at night."

47

Arliva looked at him in astonishment.

"I don't think I would run into difficulties of that sort," she replied in a superior way.

"I wouldn't bet on it not happening to someone with a face like yours," the man remarked. "If your father was here, I'm sure he'd give you the same advice as I have given you."

"It's very kind of you to be so concerned," Arliva said, "and I will certainly do as you suggest."

"There's a good girl and I hope we'll meet again sometime," the man replied. "I get off at the next station, but I'll be thinking about you because I can't help it. I'm hoping against hope that we'll meet again."

Arliva held out her hand.

"I have enjoyed meeting you very much and thank you for your kindness."

He shook her hand and shook it hard.

Then, as the train stopped, he opened the door and jumped out.

"Goodbye," he called out through the open window raising his hat. "Take good care of yourself."

He walked away and joined a number of people who had already disembarked at the station.

Arliva sat back smiling to herself.

She had at least met one man who was interested enough in her for herself and he had been kind enough to give her advice and not to think that in any way she might be useful to him.

The train moved on and they came to the station that Mrs. Hill had told her to alight at.

She got out and found a porter to take her case out of the guard's van.

"I think," Arliva said somewhat nervously, "I have someone meeting me from Lord Wilson's house."

"Oh, I knows where that be," the porter said. "'E's often been 'ere and I expects, though it be impertinent of me to say so, miss, that you be the next Governess."

Arliva looked at him in surprise.

"How do you know that?" she asked.

"They comes and they goes and it's a real joke as to whether them children'll ever 'ave any education for more than a few days."

He laughed before Arliva could answer and went on,

"The last one stays for only two weeks. As 'er be leavin' 'er says, 'I'm goin' away and I'll be glad to get back to civilisation. All of you down 'ere look as if you comes from Noah's Ark'."

"Well, that was rude," Arliva remarked.

"That 'er 'ad some reason for sayin' it," he said. "We're all a bit behind the times and this 'ere part of the country be very dull for someone as young and pretty as you be."

"Now you are depressing me before I have even arrived," Arliva retorted.

The porter laughed.

"I'm ready to 'elp you when you goes back and you 'aven't got that much luggage to start with."

He did not wait for her to answer, but pushed his trolley ahead.

Arliva saw outside the station was what her mother had always called a 'dog cart'. It was suitable for children and was usually drawn by one rather slow pony.

There was an oldish man with grey hair in it who climbed out and touched his cap politely when the porter arrived with Arliva.

"'Ere she be," the porter said. "I guessed as soon as she stepped out of the train she be the one that you was a-lookin' for."

"Good afternoon to you, miss," the older man said politely. "His Lordship 'ears you was comin' on this train and sent I to meet you. My name be Archie."

Arliva held out her hand and he took it with rather an air of surprise.

Then she tipped the porter, who said in a whisper that could easily be heard,

"Don't you let 'em bully you and you get your own way."

"I will certainly try," Arliva smiled.

She stepped into the dog cart and Archie picked up the reins.

They drove off rather slowly as she noticed that the pony drawing it was somewhat fat as if he had not had enough exercise.

There was a small village by the station in which she thought that there was an obvious shortage of larger middle class houses.

As they drove by, the cottages were not prosperous, looking like those on her father's land and most of them were in need of a coat of paint.

They drove on through what was obviously a very small town and were almost immediately into what anyone might say was the real depths of the country.

The lanes they were travelling along were narrow and in great need of repair and the cottages were few and far between.

And then they seemed to be driving for a long way without passing through a village.

Archie appeared to be concentrating on his horses, so Arliva felt that it might be a mistake to ask questions.

However, when they had gone for over a mile, she did ask him,

"Does his Lordship own many horses?"

"'E used to 'ave a lot and fine they were when we first had 'em, but them as be left are gettin' old and, as there's only the young children to ride 'em, they don't have enough exercise and that be the truth."

"Well, I love riding," Arliva said, "so I hope you will be able to mount me."

Archie looked at her in surprise.

"You likes ridin'?" he questioned, "but most of the Governesses who comes 'ere are afraid of 'orses and then fussed when the children were out ridin'."

"Well, I certainly am not a fusspot," Arliva said, "and, as I want to ride myself, I hope that you will tell me which are the best and fastest horses his Lordship has in his stables."

Archie laughed.

"Oh, well, one never knows just what to expect and you'll certainly be a surprise to the grooms."

Arliva thought it wise not to answer this.

They drove on in silence until they entered a village that seemed to be larger than any she had seen previously.

The cottages were thatched and in the centre was a Norman Church and there were also two or three small shops.

She was just about to ask if this was where Wilson Hall was located, when they turned in through some large gates with a lodge keeper's house on either side of them.

The drive was long, but at the far end she could see a house.

Her first impression was that it looked very pretty, and then, as the dog cart drew nearer, she realised that it had an almost grim frontage.

Then she saw the flowers on either side of it and she knew that it was definitely the country she had longed for when she was cooped up in London.

But there was indeed something missing although she could not explain to herself.

Archie drove the dog cart to the front door, which opened as they arrived.

She saw, standing at the top of the steps, there was a butler and she thought it was like coming home.

It was exactly as the old butler, who had been with her father for so long, would stand waiting for the guests to arrive and the door was opened to welcome them before their carriage came to a standstill.

"Thank you for bringing me here," Arliva said to Archie, "and the flowers are lovely."

"They ought to be good flowers at The Hall," he said. "We used to win every prize at the Flower Show when we 'ad one."

Arliva knew from the way he spoke that the Flower Show no longer existed.

But there was no chance to say anything more.

As she climbed down from the dog cart, an elderly footman in uniform which was too big for him, as he had shrunk with age, came to carry her case into the house.

She walked up the steps and the butler, who had not moved from his position since she had first seen him, said,

"Good morning, Miss Parker. I hope you'll enjoy staying here with us at Wilson Hall."

Arliva held out her hand and he looked at it in surprise before he shook it.

Then he said,

"His Lordship's resting at the moment, so I'll take you up to the nursery."

Arliva thought that he should say 'the schoolroom', but she did not make any remark as he went ahead of her up the stairs and she was followed by the elderly footman carrying her suitcase.

As she expected, when they reached the first floor, they climbed another flight of stairs up to the second where she was quite certain that the nursery, as the butler called it, would be situated.

It was in fact very much the same as she had had when she had been very small.

She then supposed that the children, who now had a Governess rather than a Nanny, were still isolated in the nursery.

She was not mistaken.

The butler opened the door into what was obviously a large comfortable room, but still a nursery with a rocking horse near the window.

A boy on the floor was playing with tin soldiers, while the twin girls, who were remarkably like each other, were seated in a large chair each holding a small doll in their arms.

They all three looked up when Arliva appeared.

Then the butler said,

"Here she is. She has arrived safely as we expected and you'll have to show her round the house and tell her all the things she has to know now she's come to look after you."

The children did not seem very enthusiastic at the idea, which did not surprise Arliva.

"Thank you very much," she said to the butler, "and can I see where I am expected to sleep so that I can take off my hat and coat."

As she spoke, an elderly woman, who she realised must be the housekeeper, then came up the stairs, breathing heavily on every step.

"You knows I hate havin' to hurry up these here stairs," she puffed.

"I forgot, Mrs. Lewis," Evans the butler said. "But you've managed them better than you did yesterday."

"They'll be the death of me sooner or later," Mrs. Lewis grumbled.

She turned to Arliva and looked her over before she remarked,

"You're a touch younger than I expected, but then we've had all sorts here as I suppose Mr. Evans told you."

Arliva held out her hand.

"I am delighted to meet you," she said. "And I am so sorry you have had to climb up all these stairs to do so."

The housekeeper seemed almost taken aback at the courtesy, but shook her hand and replied,

"I'll show you to your room and, if there's anything you wants, then, of course, you asks me."

Arliva said nothing but followed her into what she thought was very much a nursery bedroom with blue and white chintz curtains.

She hoped the bed would be comfortable, but rather thought that it would not be.

Breathing even more heavily than the housekeeper, the elderly footman brought her case up the stairs and put it down with a bang against one of the walls.

Then Mrs. Lewis suggested,

"I expects you'd like your luncheon now after the journey. The children usually have theirs at one o'clock, so it should be upstairs at any moment."

"Surely it would be much easier for them to have it downstairs," Arliva said. "It must be an awful nuisance for the household having to come up and down these stairs so often."

Both the butler and the housekeeper looked at her in astonishment.

"The Master eats downstairs," Evans told her.

"And so do you," Arliva added with a faint smile. "If the children are not welcome in the dining room, I am sure that there must be another room which would make it far easier than having to take the food up so many stairs."

Evans and the housekeeper looked at her as if she had proposed an uprising.

"But the young people have always had their meals in the nursery," Mrs. Lewis managed to say at last.

"That was when they had a Nanny," Arliva replied. "But once they are with a Governess then they should be downstairs. If not with their parents, then in a room which is easier for the staff and better for them to learn how to behave as young ladies and gentlemen."

Evans and Mrs. Lewis exchanged glances of sheer bewilderment.

"I never thought of that," the housekeeper admitted eventually.

"Nor did I," Evans agreed. "But then it does seem common sense. The Missus complains to me day after day coming up all these stairs. You knows yourself it's bad for your heart."

"That be true enough," the housekeeper said.

"Well, think it over," Arliva suggested, "and now I should get to know the young people I am to teach. But, as I can see how sensible and wise you both are, I am sure you will understand that, while a Nanny expects one thing, a Governess expects something quite different."

"It will certainly be easier for Mrs. Briggs to hurry up with luncheon if it was served downstairs," Evans said, as if the idea was still moving in his brain.

"If they are not allowed in the dining room," Arliva suggested, "put the food in another room and there must be plenty of suitable rooms in this big house. Then we will come down as soon as it is one o'clock."

She glanced at her wristwatch as she spoke.

"That will be in about twenty minutes and please tell your cook that I am very hungry."

"I'll tell her and I thinks what you says will save us a lot of trouble," the housekeeper said. "I've complained over and over again that these stairs'll be the death of me."

"Just think what a trouble that would be," Arliva remarked. "Surely his Lordship entertains a great deal and there must be rooms on the floor below where the children would realise that they have grown out of the nursery and into the schoolroom. We would be far more comfortable than if we had to keep climbing a mountain every time we came in through the front door."

"She's right!" Evans agreed. "I don't know why I didn't think of it myself. There be all those rooms in the West wing that you were saying yourself was rotting away because no one ever uses them."

"That be true enough," Mrs. Lewis agreed, "and it'd certainly save the housemaids who are beginnin' to hate the stairs as much as I do."

"Well, let's move later on," Arliva proposed. "I hate long flights of stairs and I feel depressed in a nursery.

Please be kind and give us a schoolroom and bedrooms on a floor where, if the children make a noise, they will not disturb anyone."

Arliva paused before she went on,

"Now I must go and meet them and I feel sure that you will help me in every way you can."

She then went through the nursery door, leaving the butler and the housekeeper staring blankly at each other.

The children were where she had last seen them and she sat down in a chair on the other side of the fireplace to where the two girls were sitting.

"I am so hungry after my long journey," she said. "When we have had luncheon, which I hope will be very soon, I want you to take me to see the horses. I understand that your grandfather has some fine thoroughbreds and I love horses."

The little boy looked up in amazement.

"You want to see the horses!" he exclaimed. "But the last Governess we had, and the one before her, used to try in every way to stop me riding because she said it was dangerous."

"I rode very fast and big horses when I was your age," Arliva replied. "I want to ride again and the first lesson you all have to learn is to ride well and then to jump well."

"We have never been allowed to jump," one of the girls piped up. "They told us that it was risky and we were forbidden even to go over the small jumps."

"Well, I am a jumping Governess!" she answered. "I want to ride and I want you to ride with me. How can we go all round the estate except on a horse?"

All three children gave a whoop of delight and ran to her side.

"Do you really mean we can go riding every day?" the boy asked.

"If there are horses, of course we can," Arliva said. "I like riding very fast, so you will have to keep up with me."

The children looked at each other and gave a gasp.

The girls no longer seemed interested in their dolls and the boy pushed his soldiers to one side with his foot.

"Then have you ridden lots and lots of horses?" he asked.

"As soon as I learnt to walk, I learnt to ride," Arliva told them. "As I love horses, one of our lessons will have to be to look for pictures of horses, many of which are now very valuable."

"There are some pictures in the library," the boy, whose name was Johnnie, replied to her, "but we are not allowed to touch them."

"But you cannot read a book without touching it," Arliva said, "and I want you to find me lots of books about horses as well as about the other subjects I will teach you."

"What sort of subjects?" the girls asked.

"When I was your age," Arliva said, "I used to pretend I was going with my Papa in a ship all round the world and, until he could take me, I used to look up places I wanted to visit in books and find pictures of them."

She paused for a moment as if she was thinking back before she continued,

"Then when Papa came home I used to ask him to take me there – and he did!"

"Our father is dead and Grandpapa's far too old." Johnnie sighed.

Arliva smiled sympathetically.

"But I am here and perhaps your grandfather will let me take you in a big ship one day which will be very very exciting and I will tell you all about it."

"Do tell me now," one of the little twins implored, whose name was Rosie.

"I will tell you what I want to do first," Arliva said, "but you must come with me to help me. I have asked Mrs. Lewis to give us rooms downstairs so that we don't have to come up so many stairs. Besides you are all too old for a nursery now that you have me instead of a Nanny."

"I miss Nanny," the other little girl, called Daisy, said.

She looked so like her twin, except that she was a little thinner.

Arliva guessed that she was the weaker of the three children and so should have more attention.

"Let's go downstairs and see if they have decided to give us rooms in one of the wings," Arliva suggested. "I am sure it's bad for us to waste our time up here when we might be doing more exciting things in other parts of the house."

"We are not really allowed in the other parts of the house," Johnnie murmured.

"That's all in the past," Arliva assured him. "We are now starting a new life together and you must behave in quite a different way from how you did while you were in the nursery."

"You mean we have grown older?" Johnnie asked.

"And wiser of course. Come on, if we don't get our own way now, it will be more difficult tomorrow."

She led the way downstairs and found, as she had expected, the butler and the housekeeper were just coming from the West wing of the house towards the centre of it.

"Have you found a new schoolroom for us?" Arliva enquired.

"We've found one," Evans replied, "but I am just hoping that you'll not do it any harm."

"You need not worry at all as we will treat it with the greatest respect," Arliva said, "just as I want these girls and the boy who are no longer children, to be treated as students."

She was smiling as she spoke and the housekeeper gave a laugh.

"Well you're a one for thinkin' up new ideas," she said. "It never struck us that the nursery was out of date, so to speak, and that Master Johnnie should move down because he's growin' up."

Johnnie laughed.

"When I get to the ground floor," he said, "or the cellar, I will be old like Grandpapa!"

"I hope you reach them long before that," Arliva told him. "Now come along, let's see what our schoolroom is like before we have a great deal to learn in it."

Johnnie and the two girls ran ahead.

Evans, determined to be in on the act, hurried after them and opened a door at the end of the passage.

It was indeed a vast improvement, Arliva thought, on the nursery.

It had been furnished as a boudoir for someone who was staying in this part of the house. It smelt a little musty as did the bedrooms that had obviously not been opened or used for a very long time.

"These will do us just beautifully and thank you for being so understanding and so sensible," Arliva enthused.

She knew that the way she spoke pleased both the butler and the housekeeper.

Evans smiled at her before he replied,

"Well, miss, you've certainly altered a few things since you arrived."

"I think, actually, I have saved not only your legs but your lives," Arliva carried on, "and please understand when I say I am dying for my luncheon!"

They laughed at this and told her to go downstairs with the children as soon as she had taken off her hat and coat.

By the time she had done so and her case had been placed in a comfortable and well-furnished bedroom, it was almost one o'clock.

The children had been exploring their rooms and the twins had chosen one with a communicating door.

Johnnie had been allocated a room meant for a man and the pictures on the walls were all of horses and this delighted him.

"Now come along and have luncheon," Arliva said. "Then we must change so that we can go riding. It's such a lovely day and I do want to see your beautiful grounds before we go to bed."

The room Evans had decided was to be their dining room had, she found, once been a breakfast room when there had been large families in the house and they had kept the dining room for luncheon and dinner.

The breakfast room was very cosy and the children were thrilled to sit at the square table in the centre of it and be able to look out on the flowers in the garden as they ate.

They were so excited at what was happening that they all wanted to talk at the same time during luncheon.

Arliva listened to them, but did not try to explain anything until she was quite certain that they would not all be sent back in disgrace by Lord Wilson when he heard of the alterations.

She learnt, however, that he was in ill-health and seldom left his bedroom.

In fact there would be no reason for him to know what was happening in his house unless Arliva herself told him what changes she had made.

She had a few words with Evans before she went upstairs to change, having sent the children to put on their riding clothes with a young maid, who had apparently been looking after them.

"His Lordship's lost interest and feels too weak to attend to what's happening on the estate," Evans told her. "He leaves it all in the hands of his manager. He just sits in his bedroom and his valet looks after him as good as any nurse could do."

He paused for a moment before he went on,

"But it's a lonely life for him and he's never been the same since his son drowned and his wife with him."

"It must have been a terrible shock," Arliva said.

"It were indeed," Evans agreed. "Now he just lets everything pass by, so to speak. It's been up to us to keep things going as they should be."

"I think you have been absolutely splendid," Arliva told him. "Now you must forgive me if I try to make the children much more interested in life than they are at the moment."

"I can tell you one thing," the butler informed her. "The Governesses as came here never taught them as much as the alphabet or else they wouldn't learn it. If you asks me, she didn't like them and they didn't like her."

"Well, let's hope they will like me," Arliva replied. "They are certainly excited at being allowed to ride."

"I thinks myself it were a silly idea to stop them, but it wouldn't do for us to interfere with the Governess as you know."

"I don't want you to interfere with me," Arliva told him, "but I want you to help me and that is what I know you are doing now and I am very grateful."

"It's like having a whirlwind in the house, I can tell you that," Evans said. "We've not had a new idea here for years and it's good for all of us to have a shake-up."

He laughed and Arliva laughed with him.

She ran upstairs to her new bedroom to change into her riding clothes.

The housemaid, obviously on the instructions of the housekeeper, had already unpacked for her.

She thanked the housemaid and found out that her name was Ann.

"You will have to tell me, Ann, who everyone is in the household and how many are in the kitchen or in the housekeeper's room. It's difficult when you are new to find out who works where."

"I'll tell you," Ann said eagerly, "and this place has been as dull as ditch-water until you arrived 'ere, miss. But now it's all buzzin' and quite different from what it were yesterday."

She looked round to make sure that the door was closed before she added,

"To tell the truth I were thinkin' of leavin' because it's so dull and grim. As I says to me Mum, it be like livin' in a tomb, but now things are movin' I want to stay."

"Oh, please stay and help me," Arliva begged. "I need a lot of help and, as you know, it's difficult to change anything that has been always done in exactly the same way, especially in houses like this."

"You'll change 'em," Ann said. "I've never seen Mr. Evans and Mrs. Lewis in such a state of excitement as they be now. When I left the kitchen, cook were talkin' of what cakes she's made for the young'uns and I can tell you she's not bothered to make any for weeks."

Arliva smiled, but made no comment.

Instead she asked Ann numerous questions which told her better than anything else what had been happening in Wilson Hall since the heir to it had been drowned.

It did not take her long to put on her riding clothes, although they were, she felt, far too smart for this place.

But it was all she had and she could not bear to leave them behind in London.

When she was dressed, she went to the children's bedrooms to find that Johnnie's breeches were rather tight and he really needed new ones, as well as some new boots.

"We will make a long list of all the things you need tomorrow," she told him, "but now let's find the horses, which is far more exciting than anything else."

Johnnie ran off ahead of the two girls, who held Arliva's hand as they crossed the corridor.

Evans then showed them a side door, which was the quickest way to the stables.

He came along too as if he could not bear to miss the excitement which he anticipated was inevitable.

He was quite right.

The Head Groom who had been informed that they were riding, was waiting with a supercilious expression on his face.

Arliva greeted him with a handshake and enthused,

"This is very thrilling for me, as I have heard about your superb thoroughbreds and, of course, I am longing to try them."

She was well aware, as he approached them, that he looked at her riding clothes and realised that she was not only smart but dressed in just the right way for someone who was used to being on a horse.

The Head Groom took her into the stables and she saw at once that the ponies for the two girls were old and slow.

"How well can you ride?" she asked them.

"Very well if we have good horses," Rosie replied. "But the Governess before you always said, as we were so young, we had to go on the oldest and slowest pony and it was very very dull."

"We do 'ave larger ponies," the Head Groom said slowly, as if he had been keeping it a secret, "but, as the Governess afore you were scared the girls might fall orf, I were afraid to suggest 'em."

"Of course they will not fall off," Arliva asserted. "I rode quite big ponies when I was their age and please, please let's see the ones you have hidden away."

They had been bought, apparently, by the children's father and mother just before they left on the ship which was to sink so that they never returned.

They had grown a little last year, but were still very suitable ponies for children who could ride without being afraid.

The twins were thrilled with them and, from the way they patted the ponies and talked to them and the way they held the reins when she lifted them into the saddle, Arliva knew that they really could ride well.

Johnnie had found a horse he had ridden before, which the last Governess had said was too large for him.

"I want this one," he said in a way that told Arliva without words that he was prepared to fight for it.

"But, of course, you must have the horse you want to ride, Johnnie," she told him, "and I think your choice is admirable.

Johnnie's eyes lit up.

Then, as if he could hardly believe his good luck, he climbed up onto the saddle.

"I love Spitfire," he said, "and I know he missed me when I was not allowed to come here."

"Of course he did," Arliva agreed, "and mind you tell him that it was not your fault you were not allowed to ride him and he will understand."

She knew that the Head Groom was listening to her with a twinkle in his eye.

He realised without being told that she was used to horses and, as he suspected, a very good rider.

When all four of them set off, Arliva would have been amused if she knew that he turned to the butler and said,

"That be a slice o' luck. We've got a real pusher 'ere at last."

"And not before time," Evans said. "If you asks me she be a real lady and knows not only a good horse when she sees one but how the children should be brought up to be the ladies and gentlemen they was born to be."

The two men exchanged glances and then the Head Groom said,

"Well, let's 'ope 'er stays and for 'eaven's sake give 'er what 'er wants indoors or else she'll be orf to London like all the rest of 'em."

"I knows what you're saying," Evans replied, "and Mrs. Lewis and I'll do our best. But you know how dull they finds it down here."

"Who can blame 'em for that?" the Head Groom asked. "We've 'ad some ghastly women who didn't know their job, but this one's the real McCoy!"

"I agrees with you there," Evans remarked.

Arliva and the children were now riding away from the house led by Johnnie.

"There's a lovely wood which we used to come in until the Governess who left us last said the trees might fall on our heads and would not let us go there."

"She would not let us ride," Rosie said, "and poor Star must have hated being shut up in the stables with no one to make a fuss of him."

"You must make a fuss of him now," Arliva told her, "and tell him exactly what you are going to do. My father always taught me to talk to my horses and that is what you must do. They understand what you say to them and like to know what is happening just as we do."

She knew that the children were thrilled with what had occurred.

When Johnnie led them into the wood, she thought that it was a lovely wood and the children should enjoy it.

"I am sure there are fairies dancing here at night," she said to find out what they believed.

"My Mama told me there were fairies here," Daisy said, "also goblins under the big trees, who live under the earth. But the Governesses we have had would not let us listen for them."

"You can come here whenever you want," Arliva promised, "but for the moment we must think of Star and Sunshine who have not been ridden until today for such a long time. When we come out of the wood, we must give them a long gallop which is so good for their legs."

"I will lead the way," Johnnie proposed. "I know the way to the old mill and the lake which I expect you will like. I have always wanted to swim in it."

"As long as it is safe, there is no reason why you should not swim now that the weather is hot," Arliva said.

The children stared at her.

"Do you mean that?" Johnnie asked.

"Of course I mean it," Arliva replied. "What is the use of a lake if you are not going to swim in it?"

"I just don't believe you're a Governess," Johnnie piped up. "I believe you have come down from Heaven to help us. It has been really awful for us since Papa and Mama died and we have not had any fun."

"Well we are going to have lots of fun now," Arliva promised. "I am sure that there must be children of your age who can come to a party."

Johnnie shook his head.

"We have not seen anyone for ages and I find it so difficult to remember their names."

Arliva made a mental note that she would find out who they were and somehow invite them to come along and play with the children.

Johnnie should have games with friends of his own age and the twins were so adorable she felt sure that there must be local people who would love to entertain them.

'It's ridiculous for them to be shut away like this,' she reflected.

They galloped over one field and then back again to the lake for Johnnie to have a look where he could swim tomorrow.

"I am sure that I have a bathing suit somewhere," he said, "but I have not seen it for a long time."

"If you cannot find it, we will buy one," Arliva told him. "There must be shops somewhere near here."

"There is a town but it's three miles away," Johnnie replied. "The Governesses have always said it was too far for us to drive there in the pony cart."

"We will have to take one of the bigger carriages," Arliva answered. "It's a good idea, Johnnie, for you to make a list of all the things you think we need which have been forgotten during these past years. Then you can add up what will be the cost of them, so that we take enough money with us."

She felt that this would be a good way of starting their lessons, but, as she suspected, Johnnie was not aware of it.

"Of course I will," he agreed. "And I am sure that Grandpapa will let us spend the money, which was always here when Papa was alive, but we were not allowed to have any of it after he died."

"He will see to it, I am sure," Arliva said. "Now take us back through the wood I found so attractive. I have thought of something special we might do there one day."

"What is that?" Rosie asked.

"It's a secret and I will have to whisper it to you when you are in bed."

"That will be exciting," Daisy laughed.

They then rode back through the wood and Arliva thought that it was a pretty wood for children.

There was a pool in the centre and she knew that they would have to learn the story of '*Tom and the Water Babies*'.

There was a little house used by woodmen where they kept the tools they did not want to carry backwards and forwards to the house.

New ideas were surging through her mind as they rode back somewhat reluctantly because it was long after teatime.

"It has been so lovely! Lovely!" Rosie cried. "Do you really mean we can really ride again tomorrow?"

"Of course we must," Arliva told her. "As you can see the poor ponies have grown far too fat with not having enough exercise. Although you may feel a little stiff, it will soon wear off, but only if you are riding because you need exercise as well as your ponies."

The twins gave a hoot of delight and Johnnie said,

"Promise you will stay with us and not go away because you are bored."

"At present I am not the least bit bored," Arliva assured him. "I am enjoying every moment of being here. But, of course, you will have to help me and we must think of new things to do every day."

She paused thoughtfully before she went on,

"But the twins must have children of their own age to play with."

Johnnie stared at her.

"There used to be children round here when I was little, but after Mama and Papa died they did not come to see us anymore."

"I expect they did not realise now much you missed them," Arliva answered. "Leave it to me and you will have to tell me their names."

"Mr. Marshall will know all their names," Johnnie said. "He comes on Thursday and Friday to do the wages for people in the house and on the estate. He also copes with all Grandpapa's correspondence."

When he said 'Grandpapa', Arliva realised that she had almost forgotten Lord Wilson whose rooms were on the other side of the house to where she and the children now were.

When they rode back, it was to find a delicious tea waiting for them in their schoolroom.

There were lots of teacakes and scones, also hot toast that Arliva had not been offered since she was a child.

It was served in a silver toast-rack and the children jumped with joy at what they saw.

Evans stood by with a wry smile on his face and, when he saw that Arliva was watching him, he winked his eye and said,

"You can be quite sure we wouldn't have carried all this up two flights of stairs to the nursery!"

"I sensed you would say that," Arliva laughed. "So please do tell the cook we are very very grateful and the children will come and thank her when they have finished their tea for all that she has produced for them."

Evans looked so surprised that she thought for a moment he was going to refuse.

Then he said,

"I'm sure cook'll be very pleased to see them."

They all ate a very large tea and Arliva found that the exercise had given her an appetite, also because it was so thrilling to be doing something different from what had been done here before.

She could understand why the Governesses before her had found it extremely dull at Wilson Hall.

She would have to find out if there were neighbours who would welcome the three children and make life very different for them than it had been.

It was, she thought, Johnnie, who was suffering the most, because in a few years' time when he had to go to Boarding School, he would find it very difficult if he had been on his own as he was at present.

Instead he should be competing with boys of his own age.

She was still thinking of what she should do next when they rose from the tea-table and Evans led the way into the kitchen where the cook was waiting for them.

CHAPTER FOUR

It was not until late in the afternoon after they had explored the garden and the greenhouses that Lord Wilson sent for Arliva.

She walked along the passage to his sitting room feeling a little nervous in case he should think that she was too young to be Governess to the children.

When she entered the room, he was seated on a sofa with a rug over his knees and she realised that he was very much older and weaker than she had expected.

When she stood in front of him, he began,

"So you are the new Governess. I hear that you are turning the place topsy-turvy."

"It is not quite as bad as all that, my Lord," Arliva replied, "but I think that everyone had forgotten that the children are now too old for a nursery."

"So you had them moved downstairs into the best rooms," Lord Wilson said. "Do you really think that will improve their brains?"

He spoke in a rather gruff but not offensive tone.

Arliva gave a little laugh.

"I hope so, my Lord, but I expect you know as well as I do that children have to be enticed into learning not forced into it."

"I wonder who told you that," Lord Wilson asked.

There was silence for a moment.

And then unexpectedly he enquired,

"Where do you come from?"

As the question came as such a surprise, Arliva told him the truth.

"I come from Gloucestershire, which is where I was born."

"Gloucestershire," the old man said slowly. "I had a friend there at one time. Lord Ashdown was his name. He made a great fortune for himself very cleverly and I wish now that I had followed his advice."

For a moment because he had mentioned her father, Arliva thought that he had recognised her.

Then she realised that he was looking back into the past and that he was more or less talking to himself.

"If I had gone into the Diplomatic Corps," the old man was saying, "like old Ashdown, then I would be a millionaire today. Although what I would do with it, I have no idea."

Arliva thought it best to be silent for the moment and only after what was quite a long pause, did she say,

"I do think, my Lord, that the children should have friends of their own age and it is certainly important for Johnnie to be in touch with other boys before he goes to Boarding School."

"And where do you think you would find them?" he asked. "When my son was alive, there used to be people coming in for luncheon, inspecting the horses and admiring the garden. Where have they all gone to? They cannot all be dead!"

Arliva knew the answer to this one was that they found the old man, who was clearly almost in his dotage, too dull to bother about.

Then she said,

"I hope you will not mind, my Lord, if I ask other boys and girls in the neighbourhood to come to luncheon or tea. Then to ride or swim with your grandchildren."

"If you can find them, you ask them," he replied. "Where are you thinking of swimming?"

"In the lake of course," Arliva answered. "I believe it will be fun for them to learn to swim and also good for their health. We can also hold a large party with lots of balloons."

"Ideas! Ideas!" Lord Wilson said. "It's always the same. Women come here with ideas, then before they have even put them into operation they leave. Too lonely here, they tell me. What do they expect, an Army of soldiers to amuse them?"

Arliva laughed.

"I expect it is what some of them expect these days, but I am sure that there are many people in this part of the world who would love to come to see this beautiful house, admire your pictures and, of course, your superb library."

"Books I am too old to read," he remarked sharply.

Arliva realised that if he had trouble with his eyes, it was a sore point.

"I have some ideas that I hope you will approve of, my Lord," Arliva said. "If they provide companions for your grandchildren, I am sure that it will make them very happy."

There was a pause and then, as he did not speak, she went on,

"Thank you so much for saying I can arrange things as I want them to be, my Lord. I don't think you will be disappointed with the result."

The old man did not answer and she turned towards the door.

"Thank you, my Lord," she said, "and I hope that I will be able to do all that I have suggested."

She did not wait for him to answer, but went from the room closing the door quietly behind her.

At least he had not prevented her in any way from putting into action the plan she had at the moment, which she thought it would be a mistake to talk about until it was in full swing.

*

She spent the time before supper playing the piano in the music room.

She suggested that the children should sing some of the songs that were popular in London. They enjoyed them and she made a mental note that she must buy more songs for them.

When the children had gone up to bed, she asked Evans,

"Where is the nearest town?"

"Now you're asking," Evans replied. "There be two, but they're each about the same distance from here."

"Which one has the best shops?" she enquired.

He laughed.

"And you should add to that, 'which are the most expensive'."

"We will go to one of them tomorrow morning," she announced, "as I have some items I want to buy that I am sure will be of interest to the children."

"When I heard them singing this evening," Evans said, "it were like the old days. Their father and mother, when they first married, would often sing duets together."

He paused before he continued,

"Every few weeks we'd have an orchestra to play after the dinner parties and there'd be dancing. Ah, them were the days. I had three footmen under me then and I can assure you they were all busy."

"I am certain they were," Arliva said. "And I am positive that, if my plans work out as I hope, you will need them again."

"That'll be the day!" Evans exclaimed.

"You wait and see. Anyway don't forget that we want a carriage at nine-thirty tomorrow morning to take us to the town."

She knew that Evans was longing to ask her more questions as to what she wanted to buy.

She slipped away upstairs feeling that, if her plan worked, it would be very exciting. But if it did not, they would all laugh at her.

She looked into the girls' room and saw that the twins were both fast asleep, each of them holding in their arms one of their favourite dolls.

Johnnie, however, was in his pyjamas, but seated at the window sketching the trees below in the garden and drawing the moon above them, which was only just to be seen faintly in the sky.

Arliva looked over his shoulder.

"You draw very well," she said. "Somehow I did not think of you as an artist."

"I want to draw and I want to paint pictures like the ones in the Gallery," he replied. "Do you think I will ever be able to do that?"

"Of course you will. I must find a real artist to teach you properly and show you how to use your paints effectively."

"I don't have any," Johnnie told her. "I asked the last Governess if I could have some and she said that it was a waste of money for me to try to paint when the house was full of pictures by great artists."

"She must have been a very stupid woman," Arliva replied angrily. "Tomorrow we will buy you paints and everything that you need and somehow I will find an artist who will come and help you."

"It sounds great fun," Johnnie enthused. "Do you think Grandpapa would stop me?"

"No, of course not. Your grandfather wants you to be clever and that means we may well discover all sorts of marvellous things you can do that no one else has achieved before. You could be a great artist in the future and the twins could be singers, dancers or musicians of some sort."

She paused before she asked,

"How are we to know unless we explore ourselves and find out what we can do that is different from other people?"

Johnnie laughed.

"I would like to explore myself, but I am not quite sure how to go about it."

"I can teach you that at any rate. Tomorrow we are going shopping and I want you to make a list of everything we need to buy and what it will cost. It is something I hate doing for myself and it would be a great help if you could do it for me."

She thought as she spoke that it was a strange way of teaching arithmetic, but surely a more useful way than merely adding up columns of figures which meant nothing.

*

The children became excited at being taken to the town.

"We have never been there before," they told her, "and it will be new and thrilling to go into the shops and buy what we want."

77

"With limitations," Arliva warned, "because if the bill is too large your grandfather might send me away as being too spendthrift."

"We want you to stay with us," the twins cried each slipping their hands into hers.

Johnnie was facing them in the carriage and now he said,

"I know what I want and that is a new bathing suit and the biggest box of paints we can find."

"That should be easy," Arliva answered. "Now I have something to tell you that I think you will find very intriguing."

All six eyes turned to her.

Then she said,

"You know the beautiful fairy wood which we go through each morning, well, I think it would be very selfish of us to keep it to ourselves. So I am going to make it a fairy wood for all the children who live near here."

She paused for a moment before she went on,

"They will be able to come and see the fairies who will be in the trees and in the grass and we will have very special ones in the middle of the wood and you must help me make it look quite unlike any wood you have ever seen before, because it belongs to the fairies."

They stared at Arliva as she continued,

"If we ask sixpence from people to come into the wood, we can then give the money to the children's home or to a school either in the village or in one of the towns."

There was silence for a moment.

Then Johnnie asked,

"Would people really want to come and see our wood?"

"I am quite sure they will," Arliva replied. "After all where have you heard of a fairy wood before? I have never heard of one, not where you can see fairies dancing in the trees and hiding in the bushes."

"Oh, please let's do it. Please! Please!" the twins cried excitedly. "We will help you, but where will we find the fairies?"

"They are what we are going to find now."

On her instructions they stopped outside a toy shop that the coachman told her was the largest in the town.

Arliva asked to see the manager and explained to him what they were going to do at Wilson Hall.

At first he was almost too astonished to speak and then he said,

"It's certainly a most original idea, miss. I think that a great number of people would like to visit the wood and take their children with them."

"And that is why you have to help us," Arliva said pleadingly.

The manager became very enthusiastic at the idea.

Snapping his fingers, he sent members of his staff in every direction to find tiny dolls and they collected a considerable number of them.

But, of course, they did not have wings as the twins pointed out to Arliva.

"I have thought of that," she replied. "I am sure that Mr. Moss, the manager, will be able to help us there."

"With wings?" he enquired in astonishment.

"They are quite easy to make and, if you can tie small bows of ribbon on their backs, they will look like fairies if they are in the grass or up a tree."

"You are quite right," Mr. Moss said, "I had not thought of that."

By the time they had finished they had collected an enormous number of small dolls.

The saleswomen were already finding stiff ribbons that they said could be tied round the chest of the doll which would stand out like wings behind them.

"We can do some of these ourselves," Arliva said. "Now we must have a great deal of tinsel, which is used at Christmas and I think some small balloons among the trees would look particularly attractive."

Everyone serving in the shop was running to bring something else that might look pretty in the wood.

By the time they had finished, Johnnie had written almost four pages of what had been purchased.

"We will take all we can work on back with us," Arliva informed Mr. Moss. "And perhaps you will be kind enough to send us the remainder of the materials as soon as possible."

"I certainly will," Mr. Moss replied. "I am thinking that you will need a great deal more silver tinsel than we have in the shop at present."

"Perhaps you will find some more stored away," Arliva suggested, "and please we need it quickly!"

"As quick as it is humanly possible," he promised. "And I do congratulate you on a very exciting and original idea."

They drove back to Wilson Hall with the children talking animatedly about what they had bought.

On Arliva's instructions, instead of turning into the drive when they reached home, they went to the Vicarage.

The Parson, who was old and who had been the Vicar for over fifteen years, greeted the children.

Then he looked questioningly at Arliva, as she held out her hand.

"I am the new Governess," she told him. "We have come to tell you about an idea that we feel will benefit children in this village and in the neighbouring ones."

She told the Vicar of the fairy wood and how if they charged sixpence for each person the money could go towards something for the poor children.

"It is the most original idea I have ever heard," the Vicar said. "And of course you are so right, Miss Parker, people will undoubtedly come from all over the country to see something as new as this. I can only hope the sunshine continues and the wood is as pretty as it is now."

"I think it's likely to be a very warm summer," she replied. "And will you please tell us who you would like the money to be given to."

"I have thought for a long time," the Vicar said, "that what we really need is a fund for sick children."

Arliva did not reply and he went on,

"If they have been ill, instead of convalescing at home where they are sleeping with two or three others and don't get a chance of peace and quiet that the doctor has prescribed for them, they could go away somewhere else."

"I know just what you are thinking," Arliva said excitedly, "holidays for sick children."

"Exactly," the Vicar replied. "If we collect enough money, we could take a sick child who has been ill with whooping cough or some other complaint, down to the sea for a week and that would be the best way of getting him or her on their feet again."

"Of course it would," Arliva replied. "I do hope we make a lot of money for you."

"Are you asking me to handle the money side of it?" the Vicar enquired.

"Of course, and we could bring our takings to the Vicarage every evening which would be much better than keeping it at The Hall."

"I promise that it will be safe with me," the Vicar answered.

Arliva rose to her feet.

"I must take the children back now," she said. "But I am so delighted that you approve of our idea. I think it will make a great difference to them."

The Vicar knew just what she meant without her explaining it any further.

Then he said,

"I have often thought that Johnnie particularly must find it rather dull at The Hall, but with the artist I promise to find for him, he will have new interests and will enjoy life more than he has recently."

"I hope so too," Arliva replied, "and thank you very much for being so understanding."

"The Vicar saw them back to the carriage and they waved as they drove away.

As he walked back to the Vicarage, he was thinking he had perhaps been rather remiss in not doing anything about those three Wilson children, who after their parents were drowned were isolated with their grandfather who was too old to pay any attention to them.

*

Once back at The Hall the children rushed into the kitchen to tell the cook what they had been buying in the town.

While they had been purchasing the fairies at the shop, the footman had obtained for Mrs. Briggs a large amount of food she required that she had never bothered about before.

It was Evans who said that the kitchen had taken on a new aspect since Arliva's arrival and in fact the whole household was very grateful to her.

"I thought they might think I was too demanding and punish us by giving us nothing but bread and water," she laughed.

"We're having dishes I haven't seen on the table for ten years," Evans told her. "And I'm not saying I don't enjoy them myself!"

"All of us enjoy them and once the fairy wood is finished I will have other ideas."

Arliva was thinking of the lake as she spoke.

She was quite certain there could be parties there where the children could have races in the water and picnic teas in the shade of the trees.

'One thing at a time,' she told herself.

*

After luncheon she went to tell the Head Gardener what she was planning for the wood. He was astonished, but gradually she made him see how important it was for the children to meet other children of the same age.

And who could resist a fairy wood even if it was deep in the country?

The next day the work started on the wood.

Every gardener and every boy who could be spared from the stables started work almost as soon as the sun rose.

It was Evans, who after a conversation with Arliva, went to the village and added a dozen men, old and young, to the workers amongst the trees.

Mrs. Lewis and the housemaids were all working at fixing wings to the dolls they had brought back with them from the town.

Mr. Moss kept to his word and a huge hamper of tinsel and more fairies arrived at midday with a promise of another hamper tomorrow.

It was the next day about three o'clock that Arliva, standing a little way back from the wood, thought that in the sunshine it looked exactly as she had wanted it to look and there appeared to be fairies climbing up the branches of every tree.

The gardeners had brought pots of flowers from the greenhouses to ornament the entrance to the wood as well as around the pool in the centre of it.

It was, however, the following day before their first visitors arrived.

They had been sent by the Vicar and they came from another Parish.

The delighted mother of four children gushed,

"I could not believe my ears when they told me that you had a fairy wood here. Of course the children wanted to see it, but I thought that it was just a joke."

"I hope you think it's pretty?" Arliva asked.

"Very pretty indeed," was the reply, "and I had no idea that Johnnie had grown so tall. He is the same age as my son who is coming home tomorrow and, of course, they must meet."

She hesitated before she went on,

"We have no lake on our estate and Rupert does so enjoy swimming."

"Then naturally he will be welcome to swim here," Arliva said.

Johnnie was thrilled with the idea.

"I like Rupert," he told her. "He used to come and see me a year or so ago and then he stopped coming."

Arliva knew that it was because they had found the place so dull.

There had been no one at the time to encourage the boys to swim or the girls to walk in the enchanted wood.

*

By the end of the week there had been dozens of visitors and their number increased day by day.

Some of them who came from the town just giggled and pointed to the fairies.

But the children loved them and ran from tree to tree counting the fairies on the branches and looking for those hidden in the grass.

Back at The Hall, Lord Wilson asked for a report every evening of what had occurred.

"You have most certainly put the cat amongst the pigeons," he said one evening to Arliva.

She laughed.

"I wish you could see how delighted the children are. Even those who think they are too old for fairies are enchanted by those in the pool. And the hobgoblins that Mr. Moss sent us are sitting on the top of the hut."

"You are a very clever young woman," the old man remarked. "I never expected this to happen here of all places and it's very good for the children to have friends of their own age. I am just wondering what you get out of all this."

"The satisfaction of knowing, my Lord, that I have made quite a number of people happy," Arliva replied.

"Quite right! Quite right!" he exclaimed. "That is just what a woman should feel."

*

One day when they had had a good many visitors and Arliva was getting ready for bed and feeling very tired, she thought,

'At least no one is worrying about me or my money and the compliments I am receiving are genuine. They are given to the fairies and not to my bank account!'

She could not help wondering what they would be feeling about her in London, if they realised why she had disappeared.

However, it did not worry her.

She was already concentrating on planning the big party she intended to give by the lake.

There would be races for the boys and men of all ages.

"I want to win my races," Johnnie piped up.

"Of course you must win," Arliva replied. "But, if you are too good as a host, you will have to stand aside and allow one or two other people to win a prize."

She sent for these to Mr. Moss and they consisted of small boats with sails that could either stand on a table or be floated on a lake or pond.

There were also prizes that would interest boys like a folding pen and other small inexpensive gifts that they could take home proudly.

When the bill arrived from Mr. Moss, it seemed enormous to Aliva and she thought perhaps that she had better pay for it herself.

Then she remembered that Lord Wilson was a rich man.

He did not appear to have spent very much money on himself, his house or his estate in the last few years.

This, she knew, was due to the fact that his son had died.

She noticed now that there were more gardeners working in the grounds than there had been before and, without making any fuss about it, Evans had engaged two new footmen who he was training and who were dressed in the Wilson livery.

She therefore took the bill herself to Lord Wilson.

"Well then, what have you been up to today, Miss Parker?" he asked when she went into the room.

"We have had forty-two visitors to the wood, my Lord," she informed him, "and twenty friends to tea with the children by the lake."

The old man chuckled.

"Things have certainly changed since you arrived."

"I am afraid that, although we have collected over sixty-five pounds for the Vicar's fund, my Lord, we have another large bill here for the fairies and the decorations we have used in the wood."

She held it out to him, but his hand did not move.

"Give it to my secretary," he said. "He pays the bills and does not worry me with them."

"You mean that you are not interested in what we spend, my Lord?" Arliva asked incredulously.

"Not really," he replied. "What you have done has made my grandchildren very happy and believe it or not I myself have had two or three visitors every day. They left their children with you and then popped in to see me. And very pleased I was to see them."

He paused for a moment before he went on,

"I have been wondering how you have such clever and imaginative ideas. It must be in your blood."

Arliva wanted to say that it was because she was her father's daughter.

As he had spoken so well of her father, she was sure that he would be able to recognise the connection.

Then she knew that if she told him who she was, it would undoubtedly be talked about in the neighbourhood.

There was sure to be a servant who had relations in London who had heard about the rich Miss Ashdown and he or she might then convey to her aunt the fact that she was living in the country and making everything different from what it had been before.

She therefore smiled at the old man's compliments, thanked him again and picked up the bill that she had made Johnnie read and add up to make certain that it was correct.

She thought now that while he had done arithmetic there were many other things she ought to be teaching him as well as making him happy by giving him companions and a chance of competing with them.

'I suppose really,' Arliva thought, 'we should have a cricket match. That is what Johnnie will play at school.'

He was not likely to go for some years, yet at the same time there was nothing that men admired or enjoyed more than a cricket match.

'I must think about it,' she told herself. 'But for the moment everything is going so well that I don't want to interrupt anything.'

The next day, however, she thought it only right that she should give the children at least one serious lesson, which she had not attempted to do since she arrived.

During the night she had found herself composing a poem about what was happening outside.

When the children had finished breakfast, she said,

"Before we go out on our usual ride, I want you to do a little serious school work we have not done before."

She saw their faces drop.

"If I don't teach you some of the subjects I ought to teach you," she continued, "your grandfather might send me away. That is why I want you to show that you are learning new ideas and new subjects as well as enjoying yourself."

Rather reluctantly they went up to the schoolroom.

"Now pick up your pencils and paper," she said, "as I want you to write a poem about what we are doing. I have written one myself to show you what I feel about the fairies."

"A poem!" Johnnie exclaimed. "That's something new."

"We are trying out new ideas every day," Arliva replied. "And this is my poem."

"There are fairies in the woods and in the flowers,
And I could watch them flying round and round
for hours.
I see them in the rustle of the trees.
I see them riding on the bumble bees.
They will float on petals drifting on the stream.
They enter all my thoughts like a dream.

They sit amongst the clouds up in the sky.
They hover near me when in bed I lie.
Fairies bring happiness and love,
A blessing from the angels up above.
All of us must pray they will come to us and stay
To bring much love and joy for every girl and boy."

As Arliva read her poem, she could see that they were listening intently.

Then Daisy said excitedly,

"I'm sure I can write a poem."

"Well, don't make it too long," Arliva told her. "Then we can go up to the swimming pool, which I know you are longing to do."

She watched the clock and ten minutes later she asked,

"Have you now finished your poems? I am ready to hear them."

"I think so," Daisy answered. "Rosie and I have done it together."

"That was very sensible of you. Now read it."

"I will read it," Daisy insisted, as she picked up the piece of paper and read,

"We love the fairies and the fairies love we.
We saw a fairy riding on a bee.
If Rosie and I catch a big bee,
We will fly to the top of the big oak tree."

The spelling was appalling, but at least the girls had tried and Arliva could only say,

"I think that is very very good. You have tried hard and have written it down well, now Johnnie what about yours?"

Johnnie, who had been sitting with his back to her, had been drawing, so she was not surprised that his poem was very short.

He picked up his piece of paper and read,

"Fairies are for girls,
Goblins are for me.
If I find a goblin,
I'll ask him home for tea."

The children all laughed.

"I suppose I will have to call that a poem," Arliva said, "but I suspect you have drawn a very pretty fairy sitting on a bee."

"How did you guess?" Johnnie asked. "But it's not as good as I would like it to be. Anyway men don't write poems."

"There you are quite wrong. Some of the very best poems we have were written by men like Wordsworth's beautiful *Daffodils* and *The Ancient Mariner* by Samuel Taylor Coleridge. But lessons are over for today and you can all run to the lake."

They had gone almost before she finished speaking and she laughed as she followed them.

That evening after she had dined alone, she went to the library and found two male poets whose words she wanted Johnnie to read.

She also found a book of drawings that she thought would help him.

Then she put them on one side and started to find the books she wanted to read herself.

It was two o'clock before she finally left, having found in the library some magnificent old volumes that she had never thought she would hold in her hands.

She left the three books beside Johnnie's bed as he was fast asleep when she tiptoed into the room.

As she went to her room, she thought how lucky the children were to have such a magnificent library, which they would undoubtedly enjoy when they were older.

'At the moment they are living in an exciting and thrilling world, which is different from anything they have known before,' she thought. 'When they are older, it will be something to look back on and remember.'

As she snuffed out the candle and turned over on her pillow, she knew it was something she would always remember too.

The following week even more people came to The Hall.

They drove in from all parts of the country and now it was not only the mothers and children who arrived but the fathers came too.

Arliva could not help being aware that they looked at her in a very different way and they made every possible excuse to talk to her.

'I must be very careful,' she thought. 'If anyone who has been in London recognises me, I might have to leave here and that would break my heart.'

Relations, who had never bothered in the past about Lord Wilson, turned up and wanted to stay, not for one night but for several.

There were young cousins with their husbands and young men who were distant relations and Lord Wilson had not seen them for years.

Mrs. Lewis had to take on four more housemaids as the relations expected to stay the night.

And Mrs. Briggs had three more helpers in the kitchen than when Arliva first arrived.

'I am a success, a real success,' she told herself one evening when they had had a record number of visitors to the wood and there were as many as nine relations staying in the house.

One of them had a son who was the same age as Johnnie.

'I am clever, very clever,' she told herself proudly.

At the same time, if there were too many visitors who were not near neighbours, it could be dangerous for her.

Therefore when it was sunny and there were a lot of strangers around she took to wearing her dark glasses.

"You look like a boogly-woogly," one of the twins said and Johnnie remarked,

"When we were out swimming yesterday, two men asked where you came from as you are so pretty and when I told them I did not know, they went off to ask someone else."

'I must be careful,' Arliva thought. 'If anyone in London has the slightest suspicion of where I am, I will have those fortune-hunters descending on me and I will have to run away again.'

The mere idea made her shiver and yet she could not help but know that it was a distinct possibility.

That night, when the dinner she had eaten all alone was finished, she decided to go into the garden.

The house party was still in the dining room and, even with the door of the schoolroom shut, she could hear their voices and laughter.

Lord Wilson's cousin had arrived during the day with her little girl of seven years of age. She also had a son of twelve who was rather overwhelming to Johnnie.

Besides he and his sister there were two middle-aged male relations staying in the house who had turned up out of curiosity bringing with them a girl of eighteen.

There was also another child who was nearly ten.

They all ate in the dining room, but Arliva had been wise enough to insist on having her meals alone in the schoolroom.

'If I have meals with them,' she thought, 'they will think I am pushy, besides they might become curious about me which would be a disaster.'

She then went down the backstairs and let herself out into the garden through a side door.

The moon was coming up over the trees, the stars were shining in the sky and there was the scent of flowers.

As soon as she had arrived at Wilson Hall, she had asked if the fountain could be repaired.

Now it was throwing its water high into the air from a cupid holding a tall cornucopia and the water was glittering with a thousand colours as it fell back into the curved basin.

'How beautiful it is,' Arliva sighed to herself as she moved forward.

As she did so, a man came out of the shadows and joined her.

He was one of the guests staying in the house from whom she had kept a distance because she was afraid that he might recognise her.

He was in fact very smart and she had heard from Evans that he was in the Grenadier Guards.

Now, as he joined her, he said,

"I expected to see you at dinner. Do you dine alone because you find our company so distasteful?"

"Of course not," Arliva replied. "But you must not forget that I am the Governess and Governesses might join the family at luncheon but never at dinner."

The man laughed.

"What an absurd rule, especially when a Governess looks like you."

She knew she was beginning to hear compliments that she had heard so often before.

But now surprisingly they were being paid to her as a nonentity and not as a rich heiress.

"I hope you are enjoying yourself, sir," she said. "It's good for the household to have visitors after it has all been so silent and empty for so long."

"I heard my relatives saying that you had made all the changes," the man said. "And I think it is very clever of you. My great-uncle was very lucky to find you."

He looked at her as he spoke with an expression in his eyes that she knew only too well.

"I am sorry to seem rude," she said, "but I have to go and see if the girls need anything. They were just going to bed before I came outside and they will now want to say goodnight to me."

"But I want to do the same thing," he persisted, "and, as I am a guest, I think I can claim first place to your attentions."

He put his arms out as he spoke and Arliva knew only too well what he intended.

With a swiftness that was unexpected she slipped away from him and, running across the lawn, she reached the side door that let into the house.

Only as she pulled it open, did she look back and realise that he was not far behind her.

She hurried inside and ran up the stairs reaching the West wing without looking back.

Only as she paused to tidy her hair before she went into the girls' room did she reflect that while she had been able to escape from London, London had come to her.

'I should have left things as they were,' she said to herself.

Even as she spoke, she knew that she had brought a new life and happiness not only to the family but to the household and to the village as well as to those who lived nearby.

'All the same I must be careful, very careful,' she repeated to herself as she bent to kiss the twins goodnight.

CHAPTER FIVE

There was a huge roar of applause as Johnnie beat the other three boys he was swimming against.

He had certainly improved extraordinarily in the short time they had been joined at the lake by a number of guests.

"Your swimming pool," one of the mothers said to Arliva, smiling, "is very much better than ours. I hope you will not mind if we turn up nearly every day."

"It's very good for Johnnie and the girls to have companions," Arliva replied.

"You are quite right," the mother agreed. "I often thought in the past that they looked rather lonely as if they were not enjoying themselves as they ought to do at that age."

It was a compliment that Arliva was receiving over and over again.

She mused to herself that she had certainly brought a new atmosphere to Wilson Hall and its occupants.

The number of servants had increased considerably and they seemed happy too. They were always thinking of new cakes and puddings to tempt the children's appetites, not that they really needed tempting.

Arliva was pleased to see that both the girls seemed to have grown a little while Johnnie was definitely much stronger than he had been when she arrived.

More and more of Lord Wilson's relations came to stay and they were obviously delighted at what they found.

They did not leave without saying that they would be coming back very shortly.

'What I have think about of now,' Arliva said to herself, 'is something special for the winter.'

The idea of producing a Nativity play at Christmas passed through her mind.

But she thought more important still that they must have something to keep them energetic, which their new friends in the County could join in.

As Johnnie and the boys he had been swimming against came out of the water, the girls were ready for their race.

They were all slightly older than Rosie and Daisy, but at Arliva's suggestion they had practised early every morning before the party and she was sure if they could not win they would certainly not be last.

The Vicar, who had been extremely interested in all that was happening up at The Hall, had undertaken to be the referee at the swimming races.

He now began to give them their orders and to tell them that he would count up to three before he called out the word '*go*' when they would plunge into the water.

They lined up at the far end of the lake.

As they did so, Arliva, looking back, saw a young boy running towards her from the wood.

She wondered why he was coming and then saw from the way he was dressed that he was not one of their visitors.

As he was running very fast towards her, she began to walk towards him.

He was breathless by the time he reached her from having run so fast.

She did not recognise him and thought that he must be from the village.

"Are you looking for me?" she began. "What is it you have come to tell me?"

Jerkily, because he was out of breath from running so fast, he answered,

"There's been – an accident in the wood to a little girl, miss, and – they wants you there."

Arliva looked back towards the lake and saw that the race had already started and the grown-ups were all cheering on the child they wanted to win.

"I will come and see what I can do to help. What has happened?" she asked.

The boy, however, was already running back.

She thought that it would save time if she went with him at once rather than cross-examine him.

She therefore hurried after him.

But he ran very quickly and he reached the wood well before she did.

There was an opening where there had once been a gate and from here there was a path between the trees that led to the pool.

As she ran on into the wood, Arliva could see the fairies dancing amongst the leaves. There was quite a lot of them on the fence that surrounded the wood, both at the front and at the back.

The boy had quickened his pace and he slipped into the wood ahead of her.

Because she thought that she might lose him and have some difficulty in finding the child who was injured, Arliva hurried after him and was rather breathless as she reached the opening between the trees.

The boy was now no longer in sight,

But she thought he would be waiting for her a little further on to take her to the accident.

Then, as she began to move forward, quite suddenly something, which felt like a blanket, was thrown over her head.

Even as she gave out a little scream of astonishment she was aware that two men, one on either side of her, were picking her up in their arms.

"Put me down!" she cried. "What are you – doing to me?"

It was difficult for her to say the words.

At the same time she realised that she was helpless.

The men were carrying her not too quickly because they were moving between the trees.

Although she tried to push the blanket away with her hands, it was too difficult to do so as the men had their arms tightly and securely round her.

She could not imagine what was happening or why, if there had been an accident, they were behaving in such an extraordinary manner.

Then she became aware that they were leaving the wood, not as she thought on the side that faced the house, but into the lane at the far end of it.

It was a very narrow lane and very little used as it only led from the village up into a farm which was a small and insignificant one somewhere beyond the lake.

She felt the men moving onto the road and then a moment later realised that she was being deposited onto the seat of a carriage.

She tried to scream for help but they were fastening the blanket at her waist and it was impossible for her even to free her hands.

Then her feet were tied together at the ankles.

Without her hearing any word spoken, the horse or horses that were drawing the carriage moved off.

She thought, although she could not be sure, that one man was sitting opposite her in the carriage and the other was in front with the driver.

'How can this possibly be happening to me?' she asked herself. 'Surely I must be dreaming.'

It was very difficult for her to breathe through the thickness of the blanket.

Although she wanted to yell out for help, she knew that it would be just a waste of energy.

The horses, and she guessed now that there were two, were gathering speed. She leant back, because she was afraid of falling forward.

She could not imagine what was going on and why she was being treated in this way.

She wondered what would happen when the party at the lake discovered that she was missing and then there would be no one to tell them what had taken place.

But the swimming would go on for another hour or so before they sat down to the picnic tea she had arranged for them in a tent.

Even then they might think that she had just gone to the house or was likely to turn up at any moment so no one would be anxious.

'Just how can this be happening to me?' she asked herself again and again.

But the horses trotted on and on.

Because it was extremely hot and airless, she tried to breathe the best way she could.

It must have been almost two hours later when she was aware that they were moving on far better roads than they had been at first.

The horses then began to slow down and she knew without being told that they were passing through some gates and were now in a drive.

'Where can I be and what can be going on?' she questioned as she had asked a thousand times already.

But there was no answer, only the horses coming to a standstill.

She thought that now, at last, she would know who was behaving towards her in this extraordinary manner.

She was taken out of the carriage and up the steps to what she was sure was the front door of a house.

Then the two men were carrying her up a staircase.

It all seemed so incredible and even now she could hardly believe that it was really happening and she was not imagining it.

Then she was put down on what she thought was a sofa and she hoped that, after she had clearly reached her destination, they would at least set her free.

Her hopes were realised.

The men began to undo the rope or whatever it was that bound her legs together and she felt, as it had been so tight, it was at least some relief.

Then she felt the rope round her body being taken away and now she would be able to breathe more easily.

Then to her surprise they did not take the blanket off her, but walked away, she presumed towards the door.

Very slowly, because she was frightened, she lifted the blanket away from her face.

Then, with a huge effort, she managed to throw it off.

She saw that she was in a bedroom, well-furnished and containing a four-poster bed.

She stared round her in sheer astonishment.

Why had she been brought here and who owned this pretty and obviously comfortable room?

She pushed her hair, which had been pressed down by the blanket, off her forehead.

She thought that she had enough strength to rise to her feet, but before she could do so, the door opened.

As she turned her head, she saw that a woman was walking towards her.

She could hardly believe who it was.

Then with a gasp she realised that she was right and it was indeed the Countess of Sturton looking, she thought, as unpleasant as she always thought her to be.

The Countess reached her and then Arliva cried out,

"What is happening? And why have I been brought here in this extraordinary manner? I don't understand."

"That is exactly what I have now come to explain to you," the Countess replied. "I expect, as it's very hot, you would like a drink of water."

She went to the washstand, filled a glass and then brought it back to Arliva.

Because her throat was so dry and she felt as if her body was dripping with heat, she drank half of the glass rapidly before she repeated,

"I don't understand why I have been brought here."

"That is what I am about to tell you," the Countess said again.

Turning round a chair that faced the dressing table, she sat down on it.

Arliva pushed the blanket that had covered her onto the floor and then tried to wipe some of the sweat from her forehead.

Then she managed to say in what seemed to her a strange voice,

"I find it very hard to understand what is happening and why you are treating me like this."

"I should have thought as you are so clever, as your father's daughter, that you would have guessed by this time that, as I am devoted to my son, I want him to be happy. And I know only too well that his future happiness lies in marrying you."

The Countess spoke somewhat sharply in a voice that Arliva had heard before, especially when she had been listening to her through the open window at her house in London.

She thought this was extremely odd behaviour on the part of the Countess and it was only with an effort did she manage to say,

"You will, I hope, not think I am rude when I say that I have no wish to marry your son and I am certain he has no real wish to marry me."

"Of course he wants to marry you," the Countess said sharply.

It trembled on Arliva's lips to add, 'because I am rich,' however she thought it a vulgar way of speaking and remained silent.

The Countess went on,

"As I want my son's happiness more than anything else and as I believe that you are the one girl who could make him happy, I am determined that your marriage will take place and it will in a few days' time."

Arliva stared at her, thinking that she must have gone raving mad.

But she saw by the expression on her face that she was determined that the Earl should be her husband just as she had suggested it to him when she heard them talking outside her sitting room.

With an effort she tried to sit up a little straighter than she was before and said deliberately quietly,

"I am sorry to disappoint you, Countess, but I have no intention at the moment of marrying anyone, although I am sure that your son is very sincere in his anxiety to be my husband. My answer is still very definitely 'no'."

The Countess laughed and it was not a pleasant sound.

"Do you really believe I will accept that? In fact I anticipated how you would behave after I learnt that for some amazing reason I cannot understand you left London and are hiding at Lord Wilson's house pretending to be the children's Governess."

"I wonder who told you that story?" Arliva asked.

Even as she spoke she knew only too well that the relations who had come to stay must have talked of what seemed to them a charming and pretty Governess who had changed everything at Wilson Hall.

Or perhaps one of their servants knew the servants whom the Countess employed. They too would talk of the strange transformation that was happening in the country.

She thought swiftly and somewhat bitterly that she had underestimated her chance of remaining as she was, so happy with the Wilson children and continuing to think up new ideas they would enjoy.

She had forgotten that her disappearance from the Social world was bound to be continually chatted about by gossips.

"I have decided," the Countess was saying, "that, as you cannot make up your mind and your father and mother are dead, I will take their place and choose a husband for you for which service you should be extremely grateful."

"I have already said," Arliva repeated, "that I have no wish to marry anyone and that *includes* your son."

"In which case I will do what your parents would do if they were alive and choose him for you," she replied. "They would understand that any girl would be thrilled to have the title Simon can give you."

"Then I suppose," Arliva said bitterly, "any mother would welcome me as her daughter-in-law, not because I am a suitable wife for her son but because my father, when he died, left me so much money."

"As we are being frank," the Countess continued, "your money would undoubtedly be an asset in any family and certainly very welcome in ours."

There was a pause before Arliva retorted in a cold voice,

"I think that this conversation is quite unnecessary. You have brought me here in a most ignominious manner that will doubtless cause a great deal of worry and distress when I am found to be missing. I therefore insist on being returned immediately to Wilson Hall."

The Countess laughed.

"You can hardly expect me to agree to that after I have gone to so much trouble taking you away. In fact to save them worrying over you I have left a note for Lord Wilson saying you had an unexpected call from London as one of your relatives is dying and has asked for you to be at her deathbed. You therefore left immediately and will let him know when it's possible for you to return."

"You had no right to do that," Arliva shouted. "I can only insist that you send me back and I hope it will be more comfortable than the way I was transported here!"

"It was the only possible way that I could take you away without you protesting or refusing to obey me," the Countess replied. "Quite frankly, my dear girl, you had better make up your mind to accept the situation without too much fuss."

"I will make a great deal of fuss if you force me to marry your son. I consider it an outrageous action on your part and one which would undoubtedly infuriate my father if he was alive."

Quite unexpectedly the Countess laughed again.

"I suppose that your father was always afraid of you being kidnapped and he would have to pay a large amount of ransom to get you back."

She paused for a moment before she went on,

"Well, instead of asking for money, I am merely arranging for you to marry my son. If you are sensible, you will agree with the least palaver about it."

Arliva put the water glass down on a table near the sofa.

Then she rose to her feet, a little unsteadily, but still with a dignity she thought her father would have approved of.

"I just seem to be repeating myself over and over again," she said. "But I want to make it absolutely clear to you that I have no intention of marrying your son or, as I have said before, anyone else at the moment."

She paused and then continued,

"I therefore insist that you send me back to Wilson Hall where I know they will be waiting anxiously for me despite the letter you sent in my name, which I consider a ridiculous act on your behalf."

"I agree with you that there is no need to us to go on repeating ourselves," the Countess said, rising to her feet. "I hope that you will be comfortable in this bedroom where you will be staying until you agree to marry my son. As apparently it is difficult for you to realise that you have no alternative but to agree to what I have planned."

For a moment Arliva could not think of anything to say.

The Countess, after waiting a second or two more, walked back towards the door.

As she reached it, she turned and snarled,

"As it is a big mistake for you not to reconsider the situation you find yourself, you will receive no food or drink of any sort until you have made up your mind."

She did not wait for Arliva to reply, but went out, slamming the door behind her and turning the key in the lock.

For a moment Arliva could only stare at the door as if it was impossible for her to fully understand what the Countess had said.

Then she knew that what she had heard was true, although it seemed incredible.

In fact until she agreed to marry the Earl, she would be given nothing to eat or drink.

She would be starved into giving the Countess the answer she had demanded so unsubtly.

Arliva walked quickly to the window and looked out. If she had thought of escaping from that window there was no chance.

Sturton Castle, where she knew the Countess lived, had been renovated rather badly at the beginning of the last century.

They had covered the old bricks with plaster, but kept the walls, which had been there, according to the family archives, since the twelfth century.

Thus it was a considerable drop from the window of the room where Arliva was imprisoned onto the ground below which was part of the garden.

Looking down she saw that there was a flagstone path round the perimeter of The Castle.

This meant that if she attempted to jump from the window onto the ground she would smash herself to pieces on the path.

Without looking at the door, she was quite sure that it was firmly locked and there was no exit that way.

There was a door at the end of the room.

She then opened it, but found that it was merely a wardrobe room and anyway it could only be reached from the bedroom.

'What am I to do? What on earth am I to do?' she asked herself.

She then realised that she was really frightened.

Because she had admired her father so much and always listened to everything he told her, she remembered him saying,

"If you are frightened and I myself have often been really frightened in my travels, you must use your brain. Your body may want to run away, but it is your instinct that will guide you and show you the best and safest way of confronting the enemy."

'I know what I will do,' Arliva thought. 'I will offer the Countess a large sum of money to set me free. Surely she will agree to that.'

As she thought of it, she knew instinctively that the Countess would refuse, realising that it would be better to have a daughter-in-law who was a millionairess who would have to stay in the family once she was married.

'I have to find a way. I have to!' Arliva insisted to herself.

Then she was praying, praying fervently that God would tell her how to save herself.

Or perhaps, by some miracle, someone would save her.

"Help me! Please help me!" she cried. "I know if I marry this man who I dislike and have to put up with his dreadful mother, I would rather die."

Equally she knew that she wanted to live.

She wanted to be with the Wilson children who by now would be wondering where she could be and having to go back to the house without her.

How could she have ever imagined that anything so horrible would be planned, simply because she had money?

"I hate my money!" she cried. "Oh, Papa, why did you leave me so much?"

She asked the question aloud and felt as if her voice echoed back to her from the ceiling.

She had run away from her money, but it had ended in her being a prisoner.

A prisoner who was to be starved into submission.

A prisoner who must marry a man she hated and she was certain that she had nothing in common with.

'If I offer them everything I now possess,' she told herself, 'I am quite certain that they would rather have me simply because my money is increasing year by year and they want all of it.'

She walked up and down her room until she was too tired to walk any further.

Then she flung herself onto the bed, still thinking desperately of some way she could persuade the Countess to let her go.

"What can I do?" she asked the ceiling.

She gave a deep sigh.

'Oh, help me, please help me, God,' she prayed. 'I cannot be so weak and feeble as to give in to the inevitable, just because, unlike other women, I have a large fortune.'

*

No one came near her and she lay on the bed until it became obvious that it was getting late and the sun was sinking in the sky.

She went over to the window to watch it disappear behind the trees.

The first star came out in the sky and it was then that she was praying again.

Praying with a fervency that seemed to make her prayers so real and so strong that she felt they flew up into the sky and passed through the stars.

But they must reach her father and he would guide her in what she should do.

'Help me, Papa, help me! It's your money that has made me a prisoner here. Although I feel like saying I would rather die than marry the Earl, I know I will give in simply because I will be too hungry to go on any longer.'

The stars twinkled back at her and the moon began to shine on the garden below.

Yet there was no answer to Arliva's question.

How could she escape from marrying the Earl?

CHAPTER SIX

At the end of the second day with nothing to eat, Arliva was feeling very low and extremely depressed.

'This just cannot go on,' she thought. 'I know that I will collapse soon and then they will do what they want with me.'

Almost as if in answer to her thoughts, she heard the door unlock and the Countess came in.

Arliva did not move from the chair she was sitting in. She just stared at her in a contemptible manner.

"I have just come here to inform you," the Countess announced, "that we are leaving tomorrow morning to see the Canon who lives a little way from here. He will marry you and Simon the next day."

She paused obviously waiting for Arliva to make a reply and, when there was silence, she went on,

"You will be married in the private Chapel which adjoins The Castle. But the Canon is most insistent that he always sees the bride and bridegroom before he marries them."

She paused for a while to draw in her breath before she added in a harsher tone,

"I consider it quite unnecessary when he is also the private Chaplain to Simon. However, he insists firmly and therefore we are taking you to see him this afternoon."

Arliva still did not speak and after a moment the Countess went on,

"One word from you that you don't wish to marry Simon and you will be starved until you become utterly and completely unconscious and so unable to argue about it anymore."

She made a little sound which was almost one of disdain before she asserted,

"There will be no arguments that you are helpless and that is what you will be if I arrange the wedding for the end of the week when you will be unconscious."

Still Arliva did not speak.

After a moment, as if she was disappointed at the reception she had received, the Countess turned round and walked from the room.

She slammed the door behind her and turned the key in the lock.

Arliva put her hands up to her face.

She wondered how much more of this she could bear.

Then, almost as if she could hear her father talking to her, he was telling her not to despair.

She remembered once when things were not going well for him he had said,

"Never give up until you are utterly defeated and that is something that you and I, my darling, must never be."

'Perhaps there will be some way I can escape when we reach the Canon,' she thought.

Arliva had the idea that it would be very difficult because she felt so weak, as, even if the way was clear for her to run, she knew that she would be unable to do so.

At luncheontime when she was given nothing to eat or drink, she thought that the Countess and her son would be gorging themselves downstairs.

It was then that the Countess came up to fetch her.

Because she knew there was no point in arguing about whether she went or not, Arliva had already put on her small hat and she did not bother with a coat or a wrap as it was very warm.

She was quite certain that they would be driven to see the Canon in a closed carriage.

She was quite right.

She and the Countess sat on the back seat and the Earl sat opposite them.

He was looking, she thought, more unpleasant and more idiotic than usual.

They drove in silence until, as they turned in at the gate of the Canon's residence, the Countess said, speaking for the first time,

"Now just behave yourself and remember that one word of protest that the wedding is not to your liking and you will return to The Castle to starve for several more days."

Arliva did not reply and the carriage ground to a standstill.

On the Countess's orders, Simon helped her down from the carriage and she felt herself shudder as his hand touched her arm.

They went in. Not to the Canon's house, but to the Chapel that was built on the side of it.

Inside the Chapel was empty at that time of day.

The Verger told the Countess that His Reverence was in his private room.

The Countess then looked round the Chapel as if to make quite certain that there was no one there.

Next she said to Arliva,

"Sit down and wait here! The Canon will see you after he has spoken to Simon."

As if she thought that she could discern a glimmer of hope in Arliva's eyes, she continued,

"I will escort him and you. You know full well the consequences if you make any protest."

Then she followed the Verger who was waiting for them.

Arliva walked past the rows of pews and sat down on a chair facing the altar.

She felt that she must go on praying even though, with the Countess escorting her son and her, it would be impossible for either of them to say that they did not wish to be married.

She knew that, if she was to be starved for very much longer, she would find it impossible to think and would then become completely helpless in the Countess's hands.

For a moment she felt almost too weak to kneel down, so she sat in her chair clasping her hands together and closing her eyes.

'Help me! Please God help me,' she prayed again and again.

She felt that she was utterly alone in a hostile world with no one to hear her.

Then surprisingly she heard a voice beside her that made her start.

A man had obviously just come into the Chapel.

And he had moved as she had into a row of chairs facing the altar.

"How is it possible," he asked in a low voice, "that someone so beautiful should look so unhappy?"

She turned her head and saw that the speaker was a man who was tall and good-looking and very obviously a gentleman.

As she met his eyes and saw the compassion in his expression, without thinking she cried out,

"Save me! *Save me!*"

He moved a little nearer to her and asked,

"From what?"

Almost as if she was hypnotised into answering the question, Arliva replied,

"I am being forced to marry a dreadful man I hate and loathe."

"Why do you not run away?" he quizzed her.

"Because," she whispered, "they are starving me into submission. I have no chance of escape."

She thought as she spoke that even if she ran away now the servants on the carriage would doubtless, on the Countess's orders, prevent her from going even a short distance down the drive.

"Where are you staying?" the stranger asked.

Because somehow the way he spoke in a quiet low voice seemed to make it impossible for her not to answer his question, Arliva replied,

"I am at Sturton Castle. I am being kept a prisoner there."

"In which part of the castle?" he enquired.

"I am on the first floor overlooking the garden," she answered, "but it is a sheer drop to the ground and if I jump, as I want to do – I will kill myself."

"Put a light in your window tonight after dark," the stranger said, "when they are all asleep."

"You can save me?" Arliva asked. "But it's a sheer drop and for me there is no way of escape."

The man smiled at her.

"I have climbed the Himalayas," he told her, "and I don't think that Sturton Castle will be quite so difficult."

Arliva stared at him.

Then before she could speak, the Countess and her son came through the door that led into the private room of the Canon.

As Simon closed the door behind them, Arliva felt something thrust into her hand.

As he did so, the stranger moved two chairs away from her.

It was something small yet hard and she put it into her handbag, taking out her handkerchief as if to wipe her eyes.

Simon came heavily through the rows of chairs to her side.

"Mother says you are to join her," he demanded in his hard rather ugly voice. "And don't say one word to upset her."

Without speaking Arliva rose to her feet, putting her handkerchief back into her bag.

She did not dare glance at the man she had been talking to, but she realised that he was not watching her but staring at the altar as if for inspiration.

'Perhaps he will help me,' she thought desperately.

Yet her common sense told her that it was hopeless.

How could she expect a stranger to take such a risk for her?

The interview with the Canon was very brief with the Countess doing all the talking.

The Canon merely agreed that he would perform the marriage.

Only when he shook Arliva's hand did he say,

"I hope, my dear, that you will be very happy and the Marriage Service I will take tomorrow evening will give me great pleasure."

Arliva merely bowed her head.

The Countess, taking her arm roughly, then moved her quickly out of the Chapel as if she thought at the last moment that she might beg the Canon not to marry her to Simon.

He was already outside in the carriage.

They drove back to The Castle in complete silence.

Only when she was once again locked up inside her bedroom, did Arliva wonder if what had happened in the Chapel had been part of her imagination and had not really taken place.

Yet something inside her which had made her beg the stranger to help her in the first place seemed to tell her that it was true and that her prayers had been answered.

When she was alone in her room, she opened her handbag to see what he had given her.

To her delight it was a bar of chocolate.

She then wondered why he was carrying it, except perhaps it was a present for his son if he had one or maybe he was on a journey that might make him hungry.

Having had nothing to eat for so very long, it was a nectar of joy and hope.

She ate it very slowly, feeling that it give her back the strength she had lost.

*

The rest of the day dragged by.

As previously no one came near her.

As she had long ago finished the small amount of water on the washstand, she was now desperately thirsty, but not as hungry and weak as she had been previously.

Eventually the sun sank in the West and the first evening star appeared in the sky.

It was then as darkness came, Arliva lit the candles on her dressing table and carried one of them to the table in front of the window.

As it had been hot in the afternoon, the windows were wide open.

When she looked down below, she shuddered and knew that, if she had thrown herself down as she intended to do, she would have been smashed to pieces.

Or perhaps she would be left to suffer the pain and agony of falling on hard stone and be crippled for life.

The moon was now rising steadily in the sky.

Although she sat at the window gazing out, she told herself that she was just making matters worse than they were already.

How could she trust someone she had never seen before?

But for some strange reason she had asked for help to come to her.

Yet, because she had prayed so fervently, she could not help but feel that God and her father, if he had heard her, would somehow answer her prayers.

It was just eleven o'clock when she was suddenly aware that there was someone on the ground beneath her.

She looked out of the window and, although she could not see very clearly, there was definitely a man down there in the shadows.

She saw beside him that there was something on the ground, which she thought seemed coiled round as if it was a rope.

Moving very quietly and peering down at him, she became aware that he was climbing up the outside of The Castle.

Arliva did not believe what she was seeing.

Then she remembered that her father had told her how climbers of the great mountains in the East could grip the bare rocks in front of them and pull themselves up.

As she stared down, she realised that was exactly what the stranger she had spoken to in the Chapel was now doing.

He had special tools in his hands and on his feet that cut into the ancient walls of The Castle and helped him ascend it step by slow step.

She held her breath until suddenly the tool he was holding grabbed the inside of the window, making a low metallic sound.

A few seconds later he pulled himself up and was seated in the window.

"You have come! You have really come! Arliva exclaimed.

He put his finger up to his lips and she understood at once that she must not say anything.

Although she was alone in that part of The Castle, she knew that he was wise as their voices might carry if they conversed with each other.

He swung himself deftly into the room.

By the light of the candle she could see that round his waist he had a rope.

Pushing the table out of the way, he pulled the rope further and further into the room until through the window came tied to it a much thicker and heavier coil of rope.

Still without speaking, he bent down in front of the bed and tied the rope firmly to one its legs.

Then he moved a large chest of drawers as quietly as possible in front of the door.

He smiled at Arliva.

"How can you be so clever and so wonderful," she asked in a whisper.

"We are not out of the wood yet," he replied, "and voices carry. You have to trust me and move very slowly and try not to be afraid."

She nodded.

Holding the thick rope in his hand, he slipped out of the window and she watched him until he reached the ground below silently.

Then he signalled to her.

She took hold of the rope with both hands and very slowly she let herself out of the window.

She realised exactly what she should do next, but she was afraid that in her hurry she would fall rather than reach the ground as athletically as he had done.

Slowly she lowered herself hand over hand trying to hold the rope between her legs.

Then, after an agonising descent, she felt his arms lifting her to safety.

She could hardly believe that she had succeeded in escaping from the prison that she had been forcibly kept in for what seemed to her years not days.

Still without speaking the man who had rescued her took her by the hand.

Lifting the ropes without even glancing at her, he started to walk swiftly through the flower beds and under the trees.

It was not likely that anyone would be looking out of the window of The Castle at this time of night, but he was obviously taking no risks.

As they made their way out of the garden and into the shrubbery, then a short distance across a field, they still did not speak.

Waiting for them on the road was an open chaise drawn by a team of four and in charge of them were two village youths.

"They've been ever so good, sir," one of the boys said, as they joined them.

"And you two have been good in looking after them for me. Here is some money which I am sure you will be able to spend tomorrow at the village shop."

He paused for a moment before he added,

"Don't forget that you have never seen me or heard of me nor my horses. If people ask questions just say you know nothing."

"We'll do that, sir, and thank you, thank you," the boys replied, clutching the money he had given to them.

The man lifted Arliva into the chaise and, climbing inside, he picked up the reins.

As they drove off with the boys waving goodbye, he said,

"We have done it and now you are free."

"How can you be so brilliant? How can you have saved me?" she asked a little breathlessly.

"You can tell me all about it as soon as we are out of here and away as quickly as we can," he answered. "I think the boys will keep their word, although I may have been seen by others."

He smiled before he added,

"Although there is no reason for anyone to connect your escape with me, they will undoubtedly try to do so."

Arliva drew in her breath.

"Of course you are right," she sighed.

"You will find some sandwiches beside you," he explained. "I suggest you eat them and they will make you feel a little better. When we stop I will give you something to drink."

"I cannot believe you are real," Arliva cried. "I think you are an angel sent down from Heaven to save me. I think I have just dreamt you and will wake up to find I am still a prisoner."

"Not if I can help it," the man laughed.

"Just how could you have been so superb?" Arliva asked. "How could you have had those special tools that mountaineers use?"

"I told you I had climbed the Himalayas," the man replied, "and it was the truth. But I assure you that it was not as difficult as I was told it might be."

Arliva did not answer and after a moment he said,

"Tell me where you want to go."

"Anywhere I can hide. The Countess will look for me and, if she catches me again, you may not be there to save me."

She thought it extremely unlikely that the Countess would dare to make her a prisoner another time especially if she went back to London.

But for the moment she wanted to take no risks.

She had been so frightened and was still too weak to take any more.

As if he knew just what she was thinking, the man said,

"I thought you would feel like that especially after such a terrifying experience. Therefore I am taking you somewhere where you can hide, if that is what you want, until you are brave enough to face the world again."

"That is exactly what I do feel," Arliva said, "and thank you, thank you for being so understanding."

"While we have quite some way to go, I suggest that you eat and we will talk a little later," he told her.

As he spoke, they moved out of the narrow lane they were driving along onto a wider road.

It was easy in the moonlight to see the way and the horses were moving swiftly.

Arliva ate the sandwiches he had brought for her.

She thought that they were the most delicious food she had ever eaten. In fact she could now feel her strength coming back to her with every mouthful she swallowed.

They must have driven for over half-an-hour before her saviour drew his horses to a standstill by some fir trees.

"Now I am going to give you something to drink," he said. "I am sure you are feeling very thirsty."

"How do you know how really dreadful it is being a prisoner?" Arliva asked.

"It is something I have never been, thank God," he replied, "but I have never seen anyone look so miserable or so desperately unhappy as you did in that Chapel."

"When I looked at you, I knew that somehow you had come in answer to all my prayers," Arliva sighed.

As they were talking, the man was pouring her out a liquid from a bottle.

She thought it might be some wine and, if she took it, because she had been starving for so long, she would undoubtedly feel very odd.

But to her delight it was lemonade to which, she thought, had been added a little honey to make it sweet.

She drank it gratefully and, when he filled up her glass again, she did not protest.

Then he put the bottle and the glass away and said,

"There is more to eat where I am taking you. You need no longer be afraid or feel that you must keep looking over your shoulder."

"I am not doing that. I have never met anyone so clever or so marvellous as you. I am only thanking God every second that you saved me."

"Forget it!" the man exclaimed. "Instead we will talk about ourselves. I have no idea of your name and you have no idea of mine. But let me tell you that my friends call me 'Ivan' and I rather think that your name should be 'Cinderella'."

Arliva laughed.

"No, it is not that."

She was now thinking swiftly what she should call herself, as she felt as if he had been in London and with such magnificent horses he could well have been, he might guess who she was.

She therefore said,

"My friends always call me 'Alma', which is easy to remember."

"It is not really good enough for you," he replied. "You should have the name of a magical person because I feel that without magic we should not have escaped so easily."

"That is what I was thinking," Arliva agreed, "and I don't know how to begin to thank you."

"You can thank me by cooking something delicious for supper when we arrive. I presume, as a woman, you can cook. I am taking you to a place where no one will look for you however important you may be."

He smiled as he added,

"Let me tell you before we arrive that there are no servants and we both have to look after ourselves."

"That is a splendid idea," Arliva answered. "You know, as well as I do, that servants talk and, if I arrive in the middle of the night with no clothes except what I stand up in, it would make a good story in the villages and ultimately in the Capital."

"That's exactly what I thought," Ivan smiled. "So while we plan your future for you we can do it without lowering our voices and looking over our shoulders and wondering if anyone is listening at a door or a window."

Arliva laughed.

"You are making it sound exactly like a story in a book."

"How do you know I am not writing one?" Ivan enquired. "And just where could I possibly find a more beautiful heroine than you?"

"Or a cleverer hero than you?" Arliva finished.

They both laughed.

"Well, at least we shall not quarrel for the time being," Ivan said. "I promise you can relax and not worry about the future, until we have completely finished slowly and confidentially with the present."

"I still cannot believe that this is all true," Arliva murmured. "I am sure I will wake up and find myself back in that horrible room where I was a prisoner."

"From what I could see of it, it seemed reasonably comfortable. But forget it. Forget everything except that you are planning a new future and have to make up your mind whether you are going North, South, East or West."

"That may be quite difficult," Arliva said, almost as if she was speaking to herself.

She was thinking that, if she went back to London, the Countess might follow her there.

Perhaps she would also have to explain why she had run away from where she was supposed to be staying with her friends without even taking a spare handkerchief.

She had in fact, although she had laughed at herself for doing so, put her one thousand pounds, which was in large notes, in the pocket of her dress.

She had not thought as she did so that she would really be able to leave her prison.

Equally, if she was to spend her money on anyone, it would not be on Simon and his ghastly mother.

It was comforting to know that, if Ivan, who had so miraculously saved her, was now bored with her presence, she could at least pay her own way to some other hiding place.

She was quite certain that the Countess would go first to London and therefore London had to be avoided.

She would also not be able to go home to her own estate that had been her father's house, which she loved.

"You are now worrying yourself," Ivan interrupted. "Stop it! I will solve all your problems later on. But now, as it is long after midnight, it is time we went to bed and I can assure you, although the place is rather small where I am taking you, the beds are very comfortable."

He turned off the main road as he spoke and went down a narrow lane.

At the end of it was a large wood.

To Arliva's surprise he moved off the road through a gateway and into a field.

She could see ahead of her a small house which she recognised as a Hunting Lodge as there were several on her father's estate.

The horses stopped outside The Lodge and Ivan said,

"Walk inside, the door is open. On the table there is an oil lamp which I am sure you can manage to light. After that there is food for both of us in the kitchen."

"Can you manage the horses without my help?" Arliva asked.

"They will be no trouble," he answered. "So do as I tell you."

"Yes, sir, no, sir, three bags full, sir," she replied mockingly.

Climbing out of the carriage, she ran into the house.

It was small but very well furnished.

Having lit the oil lamp, she carried it into what was the kitchen.

As in her father's Hunting Lodge, the kitchen was one room with a table where the sportsmen ate.

She realised that there were two bedrooms opening out of it.

She could think of nowhere in the summer where it would be safer to hide than in a Hunting Lodge.

Then, as she put the lamp down on the table, she saw that there was already food arranged on it.

There was also a jug of the delicious lemonade that Ivan had given her on the way here.

She drank a little lemonade then peeped into the nearest bedroom to find a mirror so that she could see what she looked like.

To her relief her hair was not particularly untidy and her dress, which was of light material, did not appear as crushed as she expected it to be.

'How could anyone be so wonderful as to save me is such an extraordinary and unusual manner?' she asked herself. 'He must be an angel sent to me from God and my father. No, he is far better than that, he is an *Archangel called Ivan!* No human being could be so marvellous.'

Then she went back into the kitchen as Ivan came in through the door.

"Have you now found everything you wanted?" he asked.

"I have drunk more of that delicious lemonade," she said. "I have waited for you, although, despite the delicious sandwiches, I am still hungry."

"Do help yourself," he answered. "The horses were hungry and thirsty and now we need not worry about them anymore."

Arliva sat down at the table.

As she did so, it suddenly struck her that her aunt and even her father himself might think it wrong of her to stay alone in this tiny house with a perfect stranger.

But how could he possibly be anything but the most sublime and wonderful man she had ever met?

When they unlocked her bedroom door tomorrow morning, they would find that she was not there to become the bride of the Earl.

"Now do stop thinking about the past," Ivan said unexpectedly.

"Are you telling me you can read my thoughts?" Arliva asked.

"I know what you are thinking, if that is what you mean, simply because your eyes depict your feelings. Let me tell you once and for all that you need not be frightened of me."

"How do you know I am frightened of you?" Arliva questioned.

"Because you were thinking you were alone with a man and there is no chaperone here except, of course, for the horses, who are far too busy eating and drinking before they go to sleep to worry about us!"

Arliva laughed.

"I am not really worried. I was just thinking that, if anyone knew where we were at this moment, they would think it most unconventional."

"But they would think what is happening to you is unconventional anyway," Ivan said. "How on earth did you ever become involved with such a horrible woman and her very unpleasant son?"

"How do you know he is unpleasant?" she asked.

"Well to force you into marriage is hardly what one would expect from a man who calls himself a gentleman. Actually I know who they are and how she has been trying to marry off that unpleasant son of hers for years."

There was silence.

Then Ivan said,

"I suppose she thought, as you are so beautiful, that you were an ideal bride. All I can say is that you must keep clear of people who behave in that way. I cannot imagine how your father and mother let you be caught in a trap of that sort."

"Sadly my father and mother are both dead," Arliva whispered. "And that dreadful Countess and her son took me completely by surprise."

She gave a little shudder and Ivan said,

"Please forget them! They will not trouble you in the future and you will have to be sensible enough to make sure that you are never put in such a position that they can capture you again."

"I promise you one thing," Arliva said. "I did not go willingly to Sturton Castle. I will always think that it is one of the most evil places I have ever seen."

"The people in it are evil too," Ivan added, "so I agree with you. But now let's forget them and talk about ourselves. I personally am very tired and will soon want to go to sleep."

"And I should like to do the same," Arliva agreed.

"The choice of bedroom is yours," he said. "I think that you will find the one on the right is the best."

It was the one Arliva had already been into and she replied,

"Thank you. I feel so much better now I have eaten some food. But do tell me why you had some chocolate with you that you gave me in the Chapel? I am certain that it saved my life."

"I actually had it on me for my small nephew who was coming to see me today. But as you can imagine I was not at home when he called."

"It was absolutely delicious!" Arliva exclaimed. "I could not imagine how any stranger could be so kind and have exactly what I needed in his pocket."

"It certainly seems that you were directed by the Gods in the right direction."

"That is exactly what I feel. So thank you, thank you, Ivan, my Archangel straight from Heaven, and I will keep the rest of my humble thanks for tomorrow and will now go to bed."

"I will light another lamp for you," Ivan offered, "and keep this one for myself."

He went into the bedroom and lit the oil lamp on the dressing table, which she had not noticed when she was looking in the mirror to see if she was tidy.

Then she could see the bright moonlight streaming in through the window and now the room seemed warm and inviting.

The bed was made up with dazzlingly white sheets and pillows.

"Go to sleep quickly," Ivan was saying as he went towards the door. "We will have breakfast late, about nine o'clock. It depends on when we wake."

"If I wake first, I will start cooking whatever there is to cook," she promised. "Actually, although you might not believe it, I am quite a good cook."

"I would believe anything of you," Ivan replied. "Now go to sleep. You are quite safe. Your angel who was watching you when you were praying has brought you here to safety."

Arliva wanted to reply that her *very* special angel was an Archangel called Ivan, but merely said,

"Goodnight and thank you, thank you."

"Goodnight," Ivan smiled.

He walked out of the room and closed the door.

For a moment Arliva stood gazing after him.

'He is wonderful!' she said to herself, 'absolutely wonderful. Thank you, thank you, God, in your infinite wisdom, for sending an Archangel called Ivan to save me from an appalling fate.'

CHAPTER SEVEN

Arliva and Ivan were laughing as they ran back through the fir trees from the lake where they had been swimming from the other side.

They had raced each other through the water and Ivan had, of course, won.

Now they were returning for luncheon feeling cool and hungry.

As they walked on through the trees, Arliva stopped suddenly.

She could see The Lodge ahead of them and there was a carriage outside.

She wondered who was calling and then was aware that the man driving the horses was a Policeman.

She turned to Ivan, who was a little behind her, and said frantically,

"The Police are making enquiries about me. The Countess has obviously told them that I am missing. Save me! Save me again!"

Ivan put his arm round her.

"You are quite safe," he assured her. "I promise you that no one will take you away from me."

"Are you sure, absolutely sure?" she asked, looking up at him pleadingly.

For a moment he looked into her eyes.

Then his lips were on hers.

He held her close against him.

He kissed her in a manner that made her feel as if the stars had fallen from the sky and the light of them was shining within her.

It was a long kiss.

When he raised his head, Ivan sighed,

"I have wanted to do this for a long time. I love you, what do you feel about me?"

"I love you. Of course I love you," she replied. "I think I loved you from the moment you said you would save me, but I did not realise that it was the love I have sought for so long until now. Oh, Ivan, don't let them take me away from you."

"Do you really imagine that I would let anyone do that?" he asked. "We will be married immediately, so that it will be impossible for anyone to steal you away again."

"*Married*?" she whispered.

Ivan could feel her body stiffen against his.

Then before he could speak, she asked.

"Do you love me because I am me?"

"I love you because you are the most beautiful, the most adorable and the most wonderful woman I have ever met," he said in a deep voice.

He paused before he asserted forcefully.

"If you think I would lose you now, you are very much mistaken."

"Do you really love me?" Arliva asked hesitatingly, as if she could hardly believe what she was hearing.

"I love you as I have never loved anyone," Ivan replied. "But, of course, I want to know how much you love me."

She looked up at him.

Then she hid her face against his neck.

"I love you with my all my heart and all my soul," she whispered. "And I really did not know that love could be so wonderful."

"We will make it even more wonderful than it is at the moment," Ivan murmured.

He looked towards the house.

Then he said,

"Our visitor has gone, but, as undoubtedly they will come back, I think we should leave and I will take you to my home."

"Is your home near here?" Arliva asked him.

"Not far," he replied. "Come, the sooner we leave the better."

Arliva felt that he was right.

If the Police had been told that she might be there and they did not find anyone at The Lodge, they would certainly return.

They hurried into The Lodge and she put on the one dress she had worn since she had left Wilson Hall.

She combed her hair into shape and hoped that Ivan would think she looked pretty even though she had nothing with her except what she had borrowed from him.

He had loaned her a swimming suit that was too big for her, but she had fastened it with string around her waist.

Now she left it lying wet on the floor and ran from the bedroom into the kitchen.

Ivan, dressed as he had been when he had spirited her away from The Castle, said,

"You are very quick for a woman! Now we must say goodbye to the place where I at least have been very happy."

"And I have been happier than I can possibly put into words," Arliva answered.

"You are adorable," he replied, "but then, if I start kissing you, we might be interrupted, so we must leave at once."

"Yes, yes of course," Arliva agreed nervously.

They went to the stables.

Although Arliva had said nothing, as she thought it a mistake to ask any questions, she wondered why the team that had driven them from The Castle had mysteriously disappeared after they had arrived early the next morning.

There was now only the chaise and two horses to draw it.

Ivan attached them to the chaise and then, having locked the front door of The Lodge, they set off down the narrow lane at the side of the wood.

They were now driving away from The Lodge and Arliva thought that they were escaping once again from the evil and cruel Countess, because even to think of her made her afraid and so she moved a little closer to Ivan.

"It's all right my darling," he whispered. "No one will hurt you. We will be married as soon as I can arrange it so then you need never be frightened of anyone again, except of course me!"

He was joking, but Arliva put her hand on his leg as she said,

"I love you. I love you, Ivan. Are you quite sure that will be enough for you for the rest of your life?"

"For the rest of my life and, when I reach Heaven, you will still be completely and absolutely mine and I have been looking for you all my life and now, thanks to God, I have found you."

"Do tell me all about it," Arliva begged him.

"Now I have to concentrate on driving, my darling, just in case the Police are still lurking somewhere in the neighbourhood and stop us."

As he spoke, he drove down another narrow lane.

Arliva knew that he was avoiding the main roads in case the Police were somewhere about.

She felt herself tremble, but she knew it would be a mistake to tell Ivan how afraid she was.

They had not been driving for very long when she had a glimpse of a very large and impressive house.

She was just about to ask him who lived there when he turned in at the lodge gates and down a drive with trees on either side of it.

"Why are we going in here?" she asked somewhat anxiously when she realised that the house she had just glimpsed was straight ahead of them.

"It's a place where we will be completely safe," Ivan replied.

The horses were moving quickly and they passed over a stone bridge with a stream below it.

Then the ground moved upwards into a courtyard.

The house at the end of it was even grander and more magnificent that when she had first seen it.

As the horses came to a standstill, a groom came running from the side of the house and went to their heads.

Ivan said nothing.

He merely jumped down and walked round to the other side of the carriage and helped Arliva to alight.

They went up the steps to the front door, which was opening as they appeared.

Arliva felt too nervous to ask questions.

She could only hope he was right in saying that they would be safe here.

A butler was standing at the door and behind him were three footmen in a very smart livery.

"Good morning, Your Grace," the butler addressed Ivan. "I was hoping that you would soon be coming back to us."

"Well I am here, Watkins," Ivan replied, "and I have a very special visitor with me, so I wish to see Mrs. Schofield as quickly as possible."

He paused before he added laughingly,

"But, having had a very scanty breakfast, we would first like coffee and something to eat in my sitting room."

"Very good, Your Grace," the butler affirmed.

Arliva said nothing.

"Ivan put his arm round her and drew her down a passage with some very fine paintings and some extremely beautiful antique furniture.

He opened the door of a room and Arliva saw that it was obviously a gentleman's sitting room.

At the same time there was a profusion of flowers that scented the air.

Ivan closed the door.

Before she could speak, he put his arms round her and was kissing her passionately.

It was impossible to think of anything else but his kisses and how much she loved him.

Then he raised his head and declared,

"Now you know that you are safe and never need worry about anything again."

"I will never worry again if I am with you," Arliva murmured, "but the butler referred to you as 'Your Grace,' so who are you?"

Ivan laughed.

"I thought that we would both have to answer that question sooner or later. But as it is ladies first, I think that you should tell me who you really are."

There was a little pause before Arliva whispered,

"My real name is Arliva Ashdown, not Alma."

Ivan stared at her.

"You mean *you* are the young woman all London is talking about, who I was told a thousand times I ought to meet."

"I ran away because people never noticed me, only my money," Arliva replied. "So I disguised myself as a Governess and was with some adorable children for several weeks before the Countess of Sturton kidnapped me and took me away so as to force me to marry her son."

Ivan's arms tightened round her.

"How could any woman do anything so cruel and so despicable to you?" he questioned. "I had no idea when I told you that I loved you for yourself that anyone could be so utterly and completely adorable and exactly what I have been seeking all my life."

"I would be quite happy to stay with you in that darling little house and cook your meals if that was what you wanted," Arliva pointed out.

"What I want is you and only you," Ivan replied. "But you will have a very different life to live here and, of course, in the other houses I own."

He smiled as he added,

"But when we become bored we will go away alone just as we have been this past week and only be interested in each other."

"I have never been so happy as I have been with you," Arliva sighed. "It is wonderful! Wonderful!! My Archangel. But you have still not told me who you are."

"I am the Duke of Hungerford. And now I think about it I remember once meeting your father and hearing people say how clever he was in accumulating such a huge fortune when he had started his life as a diplomat."

"He was indeed very clever," Arliva said. "But the money he left me when he died made me feel that no one would ever love me for myself. In fact I heard two people who were obviously very much in love with each other saying goodbye because he felt that the only way he could save his estate was to marry me."

"No one is going to marry you except me," Ivan asserted. "I don't need your money as I have plenty of my own and so I expect we will find people we can help who will benefit by it."

"Oh, darling, darling Ivan, that is just what I want you to say," Arliva cried. "I hate my beastly money and we will give it away to poor people. I just want to be with you."

"That is exactly what you are going to be," Ivan promised. "Now we have found each other, nothing else matters."

They moved apart as they heard the door open and Watkins came in carrying a tray followed by two footmen each with trays.

As they sat down to eat and drink the coffee, Ivan said,

"We have got to find you something to wear, my darling. I am sure that my housekeeper has a great number of things tucked away that you can borrow until we send for your clothes wherever they may be."

"They are in London at my father's house," Arliva replied. "I think that we will have to tell my aunt Molly who is chaperoning me and who by this time will be very worried about me, where we are and what we are going to do."

"We will tell the world as soon as we are married," Ivan replied. "But I just want to be alone with you until the crowds arrive to congratulate us, shake us by the hand and, of course, be envious that I have married the most beautiful girl in the world."

"I expect, actually, they will only be thinking of my money," Arliva countered.

"You are not to become so cynical. I have just as much to offer as you. Therefore we can forget everything except that you have eluded the fortune-hunters."

"They will be disappointed," she muttered.

"What we have to find you at the moment," Ivan went on, "is a gown that you can be married in and I am sending for my private Chaplain, who fortunately lives in the village, to marry us this evening."

He smiled at her as he continued,

"No one will know anything about it until we have had at least two or three weeks honeymoon alone."

Arliva clasped her hands together.

"That is exactly what I would really like," she cried excitedly.

"Are you sure that you don't want a big wedding with everyone shaking you by the hand and being envious that we have found each other?" Ivan asked jokingly.

"You know that I only want to be alone with you," Arliva replied. "I would hate a grand wedding. It will be lovely to be married secretly and to be together for as long as possible before the world outside finds out just what has happened."

"Then that is what we will do, my darling. Because I want you to look even more beautiful than you do at this moment, I am going to send for my housekeeper. I am sure she has the glorious wedding gown worn by my mother, my grandmother and indeed my great-grandmother stored away somewhere in this house. So tonight we will be resplendent to impress each other and no one else!"

"I love you, I adore you," Arliva said. "No one but you could understand just how agonising it has been when people have been running after me and asking me to marry them simply because they wanted my money and not me."

"I do know exactly what you mean," Ivan agreed. "Every *debutante* is told that if she is a sensible girl she will marry a Duke. They have all tried to get me, but not one has cared about me, only my title."

"I only love you because you are you, Ivan," Arliva murmured. "I promise you if I find you being told over and over again how grand and important you are, I will suggest that we go back to that adorable little lodge and stay there entirely alone together."

"The trouble with you," Ivan retorted, "is that you are perfect and I find it impossible to find anything wrong with you."

"Please don't look too hard," Arliva begged, "but there is one thing that I want to do and I know you will understand."

"What is that?" Ivan asked.

"I want to give a big thank offering to God who answered my prayers and who I know sent you to me to be my Archangel when I was so completely and so absolutely desperate."

"I just knew when I saw you that you are the most beautiful girl I had ever seen," Ivan answered. "At the same time there was something about you which told me at once that you are very special."

"That is what I felt when I looked into your eyes. Oh, darling, Ivan, it's so sublime that we are together and we will never lose this perfect Heavenly love that God has sent us and which, when we are married, will make us one person."

As if he could find no words to answer her with, Ivan kissed her.

After that it was impossible to think of anything of importance to say.

*

They were married late that evening.

Arliva was wearing the loveliest wedding gown she had ever seen. It was embroidered all over with diamanté and trimmed with exquisite lace.

Round her neck she had a diamond necklace which Ivan had given her just before they went downstairs.

"You look so lovely," he said, "that no diamonds or pearls could make you any more beautiful than you are already."

She did not answer and he went on,

"But I want you to shine at your wedding because it is a moment neither of us will ever forget."

"And how could I ever forget you, even if we were separated for a thousand years?" Arliva asked.

There was a note in her voice that made Ivan draw in his breath.

Then he kissed her very gently and they then went downstairs hand in hand.

She found that the Chapel, which was at the far end of the great house, had been filled with flowers that were all white.

The Duke's private Chaplain, who was an oldish man, was waiting for them.

As he began the Marriage Service, Arliva knew that every word he spoke came from his soul.

They were being blessed by him as well as by God who had brought them together.

After the ceremony was over and Arliva was now wearing Ivan's mother's wedding ring on her finger, they went to the housekeeper's room where everyone employed was waiting to congratulate them.

They were nearly all of them old servants who had been with Ivan's parents and they had served happily in the house for many years.

There was sincerity in the way they gave their good wishes which Arliva did not think would be the same if it had been a Society wedding.

Then everyone would have been calculating how much money she had, while the young women would have been jealous because she had married a Duke.

'I have married the one man in the world who was meant to be mine,' Arliva thought to herself.

She knew that Ivan was thinking the same.

They left the housekeeper's room after Watkins had said on behalf of the staff,

"God Bless you both and may you always be as happy in the future as you are today."

They went upstairs together and Ivan explained,

"I told the housekeeper that we wanted to be alone. I feel that I can undo your dress for you far better than any maid can."

"You think of everything," Arliva sighed, putting her arms round his neck. "Oh, Ivan, is it really true that we are married and that I never need to be frightened again that someone will carry me away just because I am rich?"

"You are mine, completely and absolutely mine," Ivan replied.

Then he was kissing her wildly, passionately and compellingly.

*

It was almost two weeks later that Ivan suggested that they should think about announcing their marriage in the newspapers.

"Must we really?" Arliva asked. "It's so marvellous being alone with you. Riding your magnificent horses in the morning, swimming in the lake, and oh, darling Ivan, I adore you making love to me."

"Which I will continue to do for the rest of my life," Ivan promised. "I think, my beloved, that people are beginning to gossip locally and that means that the news will soon reach London."

He paused before he added,

"On the whole it will be more dignified for us to announce our wedding than to have some newspaper or nosey parker spying us out and telling the world in their language what we should say to them in a more dignified fashion."

"Of course you are right," Arliva agreed. "You are always right and how could I ever disagree with anything you want to do, my glorious Archangel."

Ivan laughed.

"I expect that you will sooner or later. But at the moment you are the most perfect wife who I believed only existed in my dreams."

"I want to be the most perfect wife for you," Arliva whispered. "And, darling Ivan, because we have had to fight to be together, I think the fact that you climbed up the outside of Sturton Castle to save me from a fate worse than death will always be something very precious to me."

"Of course it will. In fact I will always remember how you looked at me in the Chapel and said, 'save me, save me,' and I knew I had to do it."

"We have been very very lucky," Arliva told him. "I am sure it was my prayers that brought you to me and made everything work out so perfectly."

"Of course it was," Ivan answered. "And we must bring up our children to pray just as you have prayed and to fight as we have fought for what is really worth having."

"The first people I will tell that we are married are the children and Lord Wilson," Arliva said. "I know they will be thrilled and I am not worried about them because, once the place is normal and the locals are mixing with the children and asking them to their houses, they will never be lonely or forgotten again."

She had told Ivan exactly what she had done and he thought it was very clever of her.

"You are right to tell them. They must be the first to know that we are married and we will expect them to come and stay with us when we give a party."

Arliva kissed his cheek.

"You are always so kind and understanding, Ivan. I was afraid that you might think other people's children a bore."

"If they are anything to do with you, then, just as I will think about our own children, they are perfect and I particularly want to encounter them," Ivan replied.

Arliva put her head on his shoulder.

"I think, darling, that we will soon be having a baby of our own."

"Do you think that is true?" he asked.

She gave a little nod.

"Oh, my beloved," he said. "I can think of nothing more wonderful than having your children as my children and making them as happy as we are."

"We will certainly do that," Arliva whispered. "As we have both travelled so much and realise it has made us interesting to each other so that neither of us can possibly be bored. So we will make our children travel too and they will learn things as I learnt them because as you know it makes all the difference when they are grown up."

"If the girl is as beautiful as you and the boy is as clever as we both are," Ivan said, "I am sure that we will have a very busy and at times a very difficult life in front of us."

"But a very exciting one, Archangel Ivan, and one that is full of love."

He bent forward and kissed her.

"I adore and worship you, my Arliva," he sighed. "I thank God every day that you are mine."

*

That night when he came from his room to hers, Arliva was in bed.

She held out her arms.

"Every time you come here to me," she said, "it is so exciting and wonderful that I feel nothing else matters but that we are together."

"Two people who are one. I am quite certain, my precious, that we have been together in other lives before this. If we do come back to this particular world, we will find each other again."

"That is what everyone wants," Arliva answered, "and what real love means."

"I have learnt that from you and it is true."

He kissed her as he finished speaking.

146

Then there was no need for words.

As he held her close in his arms, she felt as if he carried her up into the sky.

She knew that the God she had prayed to and who had brought them together was leading them in through the Gates of Heaven to a happiness that was beyond words.

It was Love.

The Love that is real and comes from God and is part of God and it was theirs to Eternity.